NO LONGER PROPERTY OF
SEATTLE PUBLIC LIBRARY

THE WINGED GIRL OF KNOSSOS

D1096965

SHE BREATHED "HAE, BRITOMARTIS!" IN BRIEF PRAYER
TO THE SEA-GODDESS OF CRETE

THE
WINGED GIRL
OF
KNOSSOS

ERICK BERRY

Illustrations by the Author
With an Appreciation by Betsy Bird

pdb PAUL DRY BOOKS ♦ *Philadelphia* ♦ *2017*

First Paul Dry Books Edition, 2017

Paul Dry Books, Inc.
Philadelphia, Pennsylvania
www.pauldrybooks.com

Copyright © 1933 Erick Berry
Copyright © 2017 Betsy Bird

All rights reserved

ISBN 978-1-58988-120-4

For Anne,

because, like me, she believes in
almost everything.

ERICK

CONTENTS

ILLUSTRATIONS

THE WINGED GIRL OF KNOSSOS

BEFORE THE STORY BEGINS

Long, long before blind Homer sang his songs of ancient Troy, long even before Troy itself rose from the ashes of her past and fair Helen smiled from the towers of Ilium, Minos reigned in Crete. The broad halls of the palace at Knossos welcomed traders from Egypt and from Sicily, from far Africa and rain-swept Cornwall and the savage shores of the Black Sea, and Daidalos built the Labyrinth, and dark Ariadne loved the brown-haired Theseus.

But after two thousand years of such peace as no other nation has ever known before or since, Knossos, capital of the seagirt empire, died in flames. With it died all her great civilization, and when, only three hundred years later, the blinded bards of the Achæans sang the Homeric tales for their barbarian nomad listeners, they told of the last faint echoes of that mighty empire.

Some four centuries later a civilized Greek, one Herodotus, wandering to Thebes in Egypt in search of knowledge, brought back another tradition, the tale of a mighty land called Atlantis, lost of a sudden as though sunk beneath the sea. Was the Cretan civilization this lost Atlantis? Some people think so.

These echoes died away and for twenty centuries the island and its past were forgotten. Then in our own time came the archæologists, those magicians who build authentic history out of lowly potsherds. They drew from oblivion the sounds and scenes of that long stilled, almost unsuspected civilization. Within our times, they found, beneath the stony soil of Crete, palaces vaster than those of Troy, ruins greater than those of ancient Athens, and remains of a people that was old in culture when the fair-haired Achæans, clad in skins, tended their flocks on bleak hillsides and crouched over their half-raw meat in primitive huts of mud-plastered logs.

We have learned too that many of the ancient legends were based upon truth. That Minos really lived, although the name was probably, like Pharaoh and Cæsar, given to a long line of kings. That tribute of slaves was very probably exacted from the smaller towns along the shores of the sea. That the Minotaur, Minos' bull, was not a terrible monster, but that bull games and the worship of the bull really existed, and that the Labyrinth too was a real place, though not the terrible maze which the Greek legend made it.

There is much yet to learn about ancient Crete and the Minoan people. What was their language? What gods were worshiped and in what manner? Who ruled them and for how long? And even among the modern discoveries, great experts do not agree. But enough is now known so that, with a fair knowledge of how civilizations are developed and of the needs that have been felt by people all the world over, one may weave together a story of those days that is perhaps not too far from what really happened.

CHAPTER ONE

THE SPONGE FISHERS

Inas paused a moment on the tiny deck at the stern of the boat to wrap the sponge net more carefully over her left arm. In the water it must be free to float out, yet it must not become loosened from her grasp. Under her right arm she wedged the three-pronged fork—a short-handled trident. With her right hand on the gunwale she stepped quickly over the side.

The water was blue here, blue as indigo from Egypt, sun-warmed at the surface, but it would be colder below. Her bare brown toes felt expertly for the heavy stone sinker that weighted the rope, and clasped it strongly. She looked up, one hand still holding to the side of the boat, eyes squinting against the sun, teeth flashing in a gay smile.

"Ready, O Nasos!" she called gaily and the sailor holding the rope about the thole-pin loosed it swiftly as she grabbed at her small nose.

How warm and light her body felt as it struck the sunny water.

She breathed, "Hae, Britomartis!" in brief prayer to the sea goddess of Crete as with a soft *shussh* the heavy stone sinker plunged
downward with its light cargo.

Inas kept her eyes open. This was best of all, these few instants
of quick descent. First there had been the sparkle of sunlight
above, as though one saw a million dazzling spangles against
the sun, then a dimming to a smoky white, and, swiftly, green
water, deeper hued in the shadow of the boat, and a tangle of fingering seaweed clutching softly at her ankles. But the stone cut
brusquely through that. Down, down. It was colder now. Inas
blinked. The weight landed softly on the sandy bottom.

She gave the rope a quick, single tug to indicate that all was
well, then bent, groping, her feet still clasped about the stone to
hold herself down. Light filtered palely here. A school of small
bright fishes startled by her fumbling hand sped by, brushing her
ankles, and something nibbled, tickling, at her toes. Around her,
coral echoed softly, *crok, crok,* through the water.

She worked with speed, one arm entwined in the rope, prying
with her trident in the other hand at the bigger sponges that
grew all around her. The thick ones, soft and fine, were the best.
She was careful not to break the small ones, since, left to grow,
they would be twice their present size and value next year. It took
but a few sponges to fill her bag and Inas was skillful and experienced. Then the increasing discomfort of her lungs and a ringing
in her ears warned her that her breath was getting stale. It became
almost impossible to hold her breath any longer and she began to
feel slightly dizzy. One more sponge, a huge one. She wrenched
and tore at it till it came away with a jerk that almost parted her
from the anchoring rope. Quickly she slipped the mouth of the
sponge net over the stone, gave the rope a sharp, double tug and
let it go.

Almost as swiftly as the stone could be hauled in, she shot upward through the water, eager once more to see the sun, cutting through darkness toward the light. The water brightened, broke into a million sparkles. Dazzled, blinking, she broke surface, and drank her lungs full of the welcome air once more.

A brown face topped by a tangle of black hair looked down, laughing, over the side of the sponge boat. Inas waved a suntanned paw, swam skillfully overhand, grasped the gunwale. Hands reached to help her over the side and she stood a moment on the rough planks of the deck, dripping in the sunlight.

Her sponge net lay in the bottom among a tangle of fishing tackle, harpoons, and ropes. "A good haul," someone cried. "See, that is the best sponge of today and of an excellent fineness." It was the last one she had picked. They were strange things, the sponges, slippery as jellyfishes, but left for a few days to dry in the sun they would die and the gelatinous mass rot away, leaving only the sponge skeleton.

From the further end of the boat, from other boats of the sponge fleet, a dozen men were down, divers constantly going and coming to dump their great pulpy masses in the wet salty bottoms, each haul being tallied on the tally sticks worn at their belts. Short and stocky, these men, with the deep chests and wide lungs of experienced divers, but they acknowledged Inas as good as the best and welcomed her as one of themselves. She was the more welcome perhaps because she dived for the sport, claiming no share of the common profit. Inas, daughter of Daidalos, had no need to sell sponges in the market of Knossos.

She sank down now on the little deck, let her slim legs dangle over the side, propped her back against the anchor-stone and its coil of rope. Hands clasped behind her head, she watched the flying-fishes leap from one tiny wave through the next, and

squinted into the sunlight. No need yet to dry her hair; soon she
would dive again.

Her skin was toasted a delicious brown, that hue which only
the true blond turns in the sun. Her eyes were as blue as the
Ægean Sea around her and her hair, now darkened by sea-water,
showed yellow as ripe wheat where the sun was drying it into
little blowing curls about her neck. She wore only a short, tight
skirt of blue linen, drawn in and rolled under a heavy wide belt
of bronze-studded, red goatskin. Into the belt was thrust a short
dirk of bronze with a handle of gold and ivory. This had many
uses, as defense against the deadly octopus and shark when diving, or in case the rope or net became dangerously tangled, or
even in the daily needs of eating.

Above her the clouds scudded, small and fleecy against the
deep blue of the sky. The motion of the boat was deliciously lull-
ing and the cries of the men behind her grew faint and far off.
How good the warm sun felt, how peaceful this, so far away
from the palace and the noise of Knossos, from the constant ceremony and elaboration of court ritual. Inas wriggled luxuriously;
with eyes still closed she sighed sleepily, almost dozed.

A shout from the boat aroused her. "*Shark, shark!*" that well
known call, a threat of danger but a promise of meat. She sat up,
scrambled to her feet.

Not far behind the rocking boat a sinister gray fin cut the
water. She glanced at the rope to stern. A man was down. He was
safe, however, as long as he stayed far enough below the surface,
since a shark prefers to attack sideways. Perhaps . . . Inas fingered
the dirk at her belt, but the old captain caught the gesture and
sternly shook his head, gesturing that she remain in her place.
One of the men had already plunged overboard. Shark meat was

good meat and if he could swim beneath, slashing swiftly upward at that long pale belly . . .

The little gray sail cleaving the water paused, turned. But the diver had been swift and sure. They saw his body, pale against the blue water, dart past the long gray snout—saw, following him, a dark streak stain the blue.

All hands were up now; the stern anchor raised so as to follow the beast. Someone threw a harpoon with a long thin coil of rope in its wake. It straightened out, its near end tightened about a thole-pin.

The water boiled into white foam about the boat as the great fish struggled against capture. Men grasped at oars, pulled and pushed, and for a moment all was apparent confusion. Had the boat been one of the smaller fishing skiffs, the fish would have dragged it in its wake as a hawk drags at a bit of stolen string. Then someone threw a second spear, touching a vital spot, and with a convulsive heave the shark turned slowly on its side.

Inas, dancing with excitement, found that she had been shouting with the rest. Now, pausing to go aft and lend a hand in hauling in the meat, she raised her eyes to the sky-line and gave a further shout for attention, waved arms to announce greater news than a mere man-eating shark.

"The Fleet, the Fleet!" she screamed. She jumped up and down on the small and slippery deck. "See, the Fleet from Egypt!"

At this news the shark lost its audience. Garments were doffed and waved, shouts raised from every boat of the sponge fleet, oars lifted high, mouths cupped with hands called lusty greetings to ears too far off to catch a message. Nasos, the old captain, came to stand beside Inas; he waved his cloak behind her wide-flung arms, in greeting.

Inas could hear the *ruh . . . ruh . . . ruh!* like a soft, roaring grunt, the chorus of the rowers across the water; it came nearer and nearer. She could see the bright blades dip and rise, dip and rise, sparkling in the sunlight. Oarsmen, ten on either side, crouched at the long benches and pulled lustily at the great oars, pulled with a mighty sweep. After two months away they were in sight of their own white, gleaming beaches, almost home.

A little gasp of amusement made Inas turn. Nasos' black eyes danced behind their wrinkled lids. She had, in her excitement, pinched his arm so hard that a row of little red marks from her nails showed on the brine-hardened skin.

"Oh, tell me, can you see Kadmos?" she cried. "Nasos, can you see him?" She hopped on one foot and tried to shade her eyes against the glare of the sun behind the long, sailless boats. "Can you see the boat of Kadmos? Tell me!"

"I can see the ship of the captain of the Fleet," was Nasos' dry comment. "Meropes' is that with the blue octopus on its bow, the second in line. No doubt Kadmos, his son, also is on board!"

Swiftly the boats glided nearer . . . nearer! Their course lay close to the sponge fleet. Inas reached up her arms to tighten the wet mass of her hair held by a crystal-tipped pin.

"What are you doing?" cried Nasos, but before he could put out his hand to stop her, the girl was poised, light as a sea-gull, on the tipmost bow of the boat.

"I'm going to welcome them home. I'll bring you news from Egypt!" she cried and sprang from the gunwale in a long clean dive. With scarcely a splash she cleaved the water, came up some distance away and struck out swiftly for the Fleet. Hands waved, voices shouted from the boat she had just left. The scent of the slain shark still lingered in the water—a menace because an attraction for other fish of the same breed. But Inas merely reached a hand to her belt to insure that her dirk had not stuck in its sheath, then turned all her attention to the boat ahead.

Low down in the water as she was she could still distinguish it from the others, could see the distance slowly narrow, more with the efforts of the rowers than her own, though she was a swift swimmer. For the rowers, attracted by the shouts of the men on the sponge boat, had noticed the small bright head, the slim body cleaving the water.

Obeying an order from a tall figure in the prow, the second ship of the Fleet, that one with the blue octopus, swung toward her. The dazzle of light was too strong for her to distinguish one individual from another among its crew, but she swam on, untiring.

Then a shadow loomed before her and a strong voice called, "Oh . . . hae, Inas . . . daughter of Daidalos!"

She was close, under the sprawling blue octopus whose eyes glared from the high prow of the boat. There a tall slim figure, in a red loin-cloth and with black hair drawn back into a close knot held by a pin at the neck, stretched brown muscular arms to save her from the sweep of the oars. She was yanked suddenly, dripping and breathless, from the water.

"You little fool!" cried the tall youth. "Why tempt the gods with such dangerous folly!" His hands were strong and rough on her bare shoulders. "You ought to be whipped!" he scolded, and shook her, hard, hard, so that her teeth clicked and her head snapped backward and forward.

Panting, shivering, half laughing, half tearful, she sank to the bottom of the boat. In a moment the laughter won. She brought a wet brown hand to her forehead in that salute given only to the gods themselves. Mocking, she cried:

"Hail, Kadmos! Crete sends her envoy to welcome you home,

but it is only the Greek barbarians who ill-treat their messengers. And my news is not ill, that I merit such treatment."

She halted, squinting up at the youth through wet gold lashes, then reached to twist her hair again into a knot. "Alas, I have lost my crystal pin in the water. Kadmos, lend me yours!"

CHAPTER TWO

THE FLEET IS IN

Meropes, captain of the Royal Fleet and father of Kadmos, was first to step ashore. The undertow dragged and swirled about his knees as he struggled through it to the firm sand of the beach. Behind him the boats waited, each poised with oars held for an instant above the water while the next wave rolled nearer. Then with a deep, sudden *ruh . . . ruh . . . ruh!* the oars plunged home, and the boat, riding high on the crest of the wave, came gliding in.

The crews leaped overside, splashing in shoal water, and, strong brown shoulder to curving painted plank, shoved and heaved. The blunt bow was beached, stern still awash. Once more they were on the shore of the homeland. The ships were ready to be unloaded; then they would be drawn by willing helpers, to safety, above high-water mark.

Already the road to the city of Phæstos, a short distance to the north, was thronged with people hastening to greet the returning ships. An hour ago the shore lookout had sighted brown sails to the south, then the flash of sun on wet, glistening oar-blades and the painted hulls of the Cretan Fleet. And though winds had been favorable and the boats not overdue, many were there who anxiously awaited them. Sweethearts, and parents of the men on board, merchants whose whole fortunes were risked in this voyage to Egypt, traders who expected to win much from the cargoes carried and who, almost before the ships could have left the shores of Africa, began to watch for their arrival over the southern horizon.

Quickly a small fire was kindled on the smooth clean sand. Each captain came forward to join Meropes and pour powdered incense over the flame. A prayer of thanksgiving went up to the virgin goddess, Britomartis, to witness and bless their safe return. This, to the ocean empire of Crete, was the harvest home of the year, the great voyage which, in one way or another, affected every man, woman, and child on the close packed, prosperous little island.

Kadmos and Inas waited, lingering on the fringe of the sacrificial ceremony till Meropes should be free. The captain, a striking and commanding figure, was tall for a Cretan, bronzed and wrinkled by salt winds, full-bearded in a fashion unusual among his people. The deep blue of the sea was deepening to purple under the sunset, gulls squealed, wheeling in the rosy light, and far off the sponge fishers hauled in their stone anchors and made for shore. They too would want to be present to welcome the Fleet.

Meropes turned from despatching a swift runner with messages for Minos the king, now in Knossos far to the north across the island, and smiled at Inas.

"Here is a lovely face to welcome home a poor sailor," he greeted her. He touched a rough finger to the damp curls on her neck, then turned to Kadmos. "I have messages for the governor of Phæstos, lad," he suggested. "Will you take those for me and my greetings to him? It will be hours yet till I can leave the boats."

Laughing, glad to be free, Inas and the boy raced each other up the beach. Meeting the crowd they wove their way through it. By now the throng of people almost choked the road down to the sands. At every turn Kadmos, well known as Meropes' son, was greeted and questioned. For every one he had an answering smile or word.

Inas, glancing at him out of slant blue eyes, felt a twinge almost of envy for this tall lad with the grave face, the sudden smile that disclosed big, even teeth. His body, with its broad shoulders and heavy chest, tapered to the lean hips and indrawn waist of which the Cretans were so proud. His strong and supple hands with their long fingers were brown and hard, skillful and strong on oar and fishing net. How wonderful to be a man like that, to have adventures, to travel and see the world!

Inas sighed. Oh well, she did the best she could with this handicap of being a girl. Then she remembered the sponge diving and other things, and smiled to herself. Even with such a draw-back life was eventful, even surprisingly adventurous.

Kadmos had become involved with two old women who wished to know if their sons had returned safely from Egypt. Inas pushed on alone through the gathering dusk. But in a moment Kadmos, breathless and slightly irritated, caught up with her again. He shook his shoulders as though to shrug off the questioners that had delayed him.

"Pah, these stay-at-homes," he said crossly. "One would think that the sea was all danger, the land all safety. Oh, in the name of weariness, here are more!"

Though the last fading daylight was behind them, they had been recognized by a group of merchants, hurrying down the road from Phæstos. These must needs pause and ask news of Kadmos, as first ashore from the Fleet.

"We at home are indeed glad to greet you and see you safe once more."

"I thank you." The boy spoke with curt politeness. "And we from afar are glad, once more, to find Crete safe on our return."

He gestured them toward the beach, where fuller news awaited them, and once more caught up with Inas. They were almost alone now on the road toward the lights of the town above them. He slowed his pace to match hers.

"Kadmos," the girl put her hand on his arm, "how strangely you spoke to those men. As though," she paused, seeking a phrase, "as though you were really concerned for our safety, here in Crete."

"We are indeed concerned, we who sail the seas."

"But it is you who have entered the life of danger; we are secure at home. Crete is as safe as the mountains that guard her. She has always been here and always will be."

Kadmos laughed scornfully, almost with bitterness. "Ask the sailor who sails to far cities . . . he will tell you that no place, left unguarded, or armed only with hired soldiers whose wives and homes are elsewhere, is safe. Ask the sailor who enters last year's port and finds only the smoking ruins of a once prosperous town, a reeking charnel-house left by the pirates' raid."

Inas gasped, then ran a few steps to catch up with him. "They would not dare!" she declared loyally. "All the world has fear of Minos. All people know the long and powerful arm of his revenge!"

"His ships," stated Kadmos flatly, "are his arms. And when his ships sail overseas, heavy with trade for foreign ports, then he is left unarmed."

Inas pondered on this. Was it true? Could Kadmos be right? But the boy sought clumsily to swing the talk into a lighter channel.

"Tell me, is all well at Knossos? And you, why are you in Phæs-tos? And with the sponge fleet?"

"Nasos, captain of the sponge fishers, is married to the sister of Teeta, my Egyptian nurse, whom you remember. I return tomor-row to Knossos, or at least part of the way. And you, when will you leave Phæstos?"

"Meropes' chariot is with the innkeeper at the city there." He nodded toward the houses they were approaching. "I leave at sunrise." He glanced at her sideways, as though about to put a question, but Inas spoke first.

"A chariot? With horses? Oh, then may I go with you? Not all the way, but as far as the rocks at the base of Mount Iuctus." And, as the boy nodded pleased assent, "Father stays there in our small house. There is the shepherd, Glos, to cook his meals when I am here in Phæstos. He . . . he makes sacrifice to Helchanos, the cock god, these four days."

Kadmos frowned. "Inas, tell me the truth. It is not for the sacrifice your father stays there. All know he is careless of the gods. Or has he perhaps changed heart since the Fleet sailed for Egypt?"

Inas chuckled amusedly. "You are too clever, Kadmos. No, he has not changed heart. Tomorrow I will tell you. Tonight . . . I would hasten home. Sponge diving is hungry work."

Kadmos would have urged her to wait for Meropes at the inn, that they might have their evening meal together, but she reminded him that he had messages for the governor of the town. "And Nasos' wife will be waiting for me."

The wide road branched here and in the fork was the inn, where the innkeeper, aware of the Fleet's arrival, scurried about, making all ready for the arriving sailors.

"Then I shall stop here and find such fresh garments as were left in the innkeeper's care," Kadmos told her. "And make ready to see the governor. Tomorrow at sunrise I shall look for you."

And with that arrangement they said good night, Kadmos' hand clinging lightly for a moment to the hand of Inas.

CHAPTER THREE

WITH CHARIOT WHEELS

The air was gray and chilly; the sun still far below the edge of Mount Iuctus to the east. Inas shivered, waiting, wrapped in a long, gray wool cloak. Beneath her arm, covered by a cloth, was a flat cake of bread, cheese, and a leather bottle of sweet wine.

There was a far off murmur that grew into the clatter of unshod hoofs. Through the milky light appeared the chariot, with Kadmos behind two small, active white ponies. He drew up in a whirl of powdery dust, reached down one arm, and Inas sprang to his side into the wickerwork vehicle. With scarcely a pause they were off again to the merry rhythm of the horses' hoofs.

"They are fat from little exercise," Kadmos remarked, "but very strong. I should reach the palace well before night. Is your coat a warm one?"

Inas nodded, speechless but with starry eyes and glowing cheeks. There was a rush of wind through her streaming hair, a pleasant smell of dew-wet herbs along the road. The travelers made a quick descent into a small valley where the night mists clung, damp and chill, then a rise into warmer air, beginning to turn rosy with the dawn. She looked up at the boy beside her and smiled her delight.

Kadmos suggested that she put her bundle on the floor of the chariot. This gave her freedom to cling with both hands to the steadying-rail in front of her. The ponies quickened their pace.

Only twice before had she ridden behind horses. Meropes had brought a pair of these strange animals all the way from Egypt. Daidalos, her father, lived in too simple a fashion for such ostentation; mules, oxen, and donkeys were the usual mode of transportation. Even now dozens of patient, shaggy-coated little beasts were being laden for the long, slow trip across the island, from the port to Knossos, a trip that Kadmos with his swift steeds would make in a single day.

The air was warming and to their left sunlight showed on the distant mountain-girdled plain of Messara, but for an hour or more they drove in the shadow of Mount Iuctus. Sunlight slid down the olive slopes, silvery green to the west, and Kadmos pulled the horses to an easier gait.

Inas dropped her cloak to the bottom of the chariot and put her hands experimentally on the leather reins. Kadmos smiled and nodded his agreement, letting the lines slip into her fingers. For a moment the ponies feeling the new hand that held them quickened their steps again, but Inas' wrists were as strong as Kadmos' and as steady. He nodded approval of her ability.

"You would make a good horseman," he told her, to her delight.

Today she wore high boots of white leather, laced with thongs, to just below the knee. A short kilt of white linen was tightened by the wide belt of red goatskin which held her short knife, and, for warmth, a short-sleeved blouse drawn in by the belt and embroidered with red and gilt threads at the neck. Her hair had been arranged in five formal curls, three at the back, one before each ear, and above the short fringe of stiff little ringlets on her forehead was a ribbon binding the locks into place. Catching Kadmos' approving eyes upon her, she volunteered news of the city.

"Your Fleet will be royally welcomed. The spring bull-vaulting merely awaits its arrival. Even now, since the word must have reached Knossos before dawn, they will begin to put up the fair booths along the river banks, and will gather flowers for the great arena."

A little scar on her cheek deepened to a dimple. Obviously this was not all her news.

Kadmos chuckled. "Tell me the rest."

"I . . . I, myself, am entered in the bull-vaulting."

"Inas! *No!*"

"Yes." Inas tried not to let her voice sound too pleased, too exultant. There was at least some adventure even to staying home in Crete. "I have worked hard during this distant voyage of yours, and when the games are finished I shall no longer be in the novice class."

It was a difficult sport, this bull-vaulting; one which challenged the most ambitious youths of Crete. Almost as soon as she could walk Inas had started to become accustomed to the bulls, had seen the games, had listened to tales of other bull-vaulters. Years of training had made her body as strong and sturdy as a young tree and always before meeting the bull in the ring at one of the periodic festivals, there were additional weeks of training, of particular diet and care. In addition the bull-vaulters were carefully selected for skill, for courage, even for grace. It was no empty honor to be chosen for this great festival.

Abruptly Kadmos reached to take the reins from her hand. Inas regarded her loss with a little grimace, then shrugged one shoulder. Perhaps one should not expect a sailor to understand a landsman's game! But even if he were afraid for her, he should not forbid her appearing in the arena.

Kadmos' knuckles showed white through the skin as he grasped the lines, but his voice was deep and steady.

"No! Inas, you are not to be in the bull-vaulting!"

Inas threw up her chin. "Let us not quarrel over that. Minos has already approved of the list of contestants, and my father has always known that I, too, would someday appear in the public games, even as he did. I am entered for all three days, and we shall sit together, all the girls in the Princess Ariadne's box."

Kadmos' black brows met in a frown. Inas glanced mischievously at him, then seeing his distress put a small brown hand on his shoulder.

"Do not worry, my almost-brother. I have no fear. Remember, I have played with the bulls almost since I left the arms of Teeta, my nurse. There is little real danger. Indeed," she confessed suddenly, "I shall love it. All the faces, the whole town, people from afar, even from Rhodes and from all the small islands, gazing down toward one. The court in its finest gowns and jewels, Minos with his feathered head-dress, and the perfumes and the flowers, the sunlight and the sighing of the fans. Then the great bull charging in—"

"Stop!" Kadmos' voice was harsh with command. "I shall be there, and I shall pray for you. But do not make it more difficult now."

"Kadmos! You have been too long in Egypt, you are softened from the heat of the sun!" She giggled, then sobered to meet his mood. "But I have many troubles. May I tell them to you? Yes? . . . It is concerning Daidalos. You see—" She hesitated, loathe perhaps to put her fears into more solid form. "They say . . . those people of the town who would cause him trouble . . . that he plays with black magic, back here in the hills. That he summons gods from the nether world, demons out of hell, to teach him their evil wisdom. And during this last moon the murmurs grow against him. Kres, the Egyptian, is behind some of this, I know."

"And is he?" asked Kadmos.

"Is he what? Playing with black magic? How foolish you are! It is but those wings he uses. We have tried to hide our experiments in the hills. And Glos, as you know, is secret as the sea. But some others of the shepherds may have seen us, and gossip spreads like fire through dry grass."

Kadmos let the horses slow to a walk. "But what is he really doing?" was his puzzled inquiry. "Wings? Only the birds have wings. The gods have decreed it so."

"Father has studied the birds and thinks that they are not so different from man. Last year we experimented with linen, stretched over frames of split bamboo and tied with fine cord. These we feathered, like wings. At first we had little success, but we have made other models and of late we have a new one, with a tail and with no joints in the wings, that lifts us off the ground."

"You fly! But that is indeed magic, though not, perhaps, black."

"You are as simple as the herdsmen. We do not fly, we but leap into the air, glide with the wind. It is as though your arms were longer and wider and spread flat at the ends instead of having hands on them. One goes no great distance, it is true, and Father is much discouraged. But I have shown him that birds do not always flap their wings. Often they also glide on the wind."

"And *you* use these . . . wings?"

"Of course! And you too shall try it someday."

"The gods forbid," he said piously. "Inas, what mad adventure will be your next? This is worse than the bull-vaulting."

Now the sun rose, bright and cloudless above the snow-crowned peak of Mount Iuctus, and the road, which had been climbing steadily, flattened along the wide plain before them. Ahead was a small, stone guard-post, the first of those which dotted the royal highway.

"Hail, brother!" called Kadmos. "Hail to thee in the dawn!"

"Hail, brother!" came the sleepy voice of the guard. "Greetings, and good journey." A grizzled face, unshaven and only half awake, peered through the small, high window; then, recognizing the boy cried, "The Fleet is in?"

"Even so." Then in a whisper to Inas, "Shall we draw rein?" Inas shook her head.

Kadmos, quickening pace, swept by the sentry and down the dusty road.

"Soon we shall stop for food," directed the girl. "There is a clear spring with good cold water near here. And I have wine to mingle with it, and bread and cheese."

Some fifty paces back from the road, high on a bank that was green with moss, where ferns grew and asphodel flowered into spiky blooms, they saw the spring. Kadmos tethered the horses with their reins about a heavy stone; then climbed, close behind Inas, to kneel by the little trickle of cool water.

With dripping chin he raised his head from the long drink and exclaimed, "By Rhea, that was good!" and a moment later told her, "That is one hardship of the sea, the sour and unpleasant taste of water after it has lain for weeks in the skins."

Inas, with her mouth full of bread and cheese, murmured sympathetically.

"Goatskins!" Kadmos' mouth twisted wryly. "And on this voyage they were old and by the time we reached Egypt they had split. We purchased new ones in the market, too new, faugh! All the water tasted of goat. Another cup of that wine, to wash the memory from my tongue."

Inas laughed and poured the purple juice into a leather cup, then mixed water with it. "But you had wine also?"

"Yes, the wine of Thebes is excellent. And Pharaoh sent some twenty jars of his finest as a gift for the king. I would like to sample that."

Gazing back over the road they had come, they slowly ate the simple meal. Behind them, to the west, pale now in the morning light, sprawled the great city of Phæstos on its rocky knoll, and beyond that the sea, sparkling, blue, stretching to distant, unknown horizons. Before them Ida rose, hollowed with countless sacred caves, and in the east Mount Iuctus, snow-topped, the birthplace of the gods.

Kadmos sprawled back among the short ferns and blinked lazily through half closed eyelids. "I saw hair such as yours in the city of Thebes. They told me the man was a Greek, from the north."

Inas looked down, threw a curl over her shoulder. "My mother had hair like this. Father says she was very beautiful."

"You never saw her?" asked the boy.

Inas shook her head. "I do not remember." Then, with seem-ing irrelevance, "Kadmos, the Greeks are in."

"What? Are they really?" He sat up, wide awake now with interest. "Then they will be used in the bull-vaulting? Do you know, I have never seen them. Last time, ten years ago, when I was but seven, Father and I were in Rhodes." Then, noting her expression, "Oh, I have hurt you! Your mother was a Greek!"

"Yes." Inas picked a spray of asphodel and seemed to examine it closely. "She was a slave. Father saw her before the auction and asked for her. Minos was pleased with him then because Daidalos had made some improvements in the palace theater, so gave him Mother for a gift. But she was always homesick for her own peo-ple, Teeta tells me."

She whipped the flower across her flattened palm, stripping it of its petals. "Father means not to be at the bull-vaulting. He thinks—"

"Yes, what does he think?"

"He says a nation grows weak when it forgets to play its own games and is content to watch the play of hired performers." She laughed and tossed away the stripped stalk. "But it is not bad to be among those paid ones. Poor father! He is angry too, about the hiring of mercenaries from the south, black men, to enlarge our army."

"Your father is wise. I, who have voyaged—"

"Pooh, always so boastful! Sailors were ever braggarts! I too shall have adventures someday, shall sail far off in a boat . . . per-haps my own."

Kadmos' brows met again. "My wife must be satisfied to stay at home, like wives of other sailors. How can I be content in Thebes or Rhodes or far off Sicily if my wife is not safe here at home in Crete?"

Inas threw back her curls with an impatient hand. "And only last night you told me Crete herself was not so safe. Besides, I'm not so sure I wish to marry you, or anyone. Why should I forgo all adventures? See, I am strong as any boy."

She sprang to her feet and danced teasingly ahead of him down the slope. Kadmos, delaying to pick up the leather bottle and the remains of the meal, saw her turn the race into a whirl of wild cart-wheels, down, down to the road. She came upright, flushed and impish, curls on end, beside the startled ponies.

Laughing ruefully he followed her. This girl was like no other he had ever seen, far-traveled though he was.

CHAPTER FOUR

RIDERS OF THE WIND

The sun was nearly overhead, the sky a blazing arch of blue, but the wind blew cool from distant, snow-clad peaks, when Inas parted from Kadmos. The boy watched the little figure leap lightly up the scrubby slope toward a band of trees that hid the hut of Glos, the shepherd, watched her turn twice and wave a farewell before she disappeared into the shadow of the woods. Her white garments gave a final glimmer, as though she had turned a third time, then they were hidden by the trees. Kadmos chirruped to his horses. Knossos still lay far ahead.

Inas, with folded cloak over one shoulder, walked swiftly through the belt of trees, climbed a stone-strewn meadow where the sheep-nibbled grass was dotted with bright flowers, and hesitated a moment to look and listen. The road was no longer in sight, but she caught the whisper of thudding hoofs above the murmuring tinkle of sheep-bells.

She reached the hut and paused to glance around. A small house of rough stone with a roof of thatching, a rude dirt floor— it was quite empty of anyone save an old cat who *prrred* and leaped down from a table to come and rub against Inas' legs. The cat had been given her years ago by the Princess Ariadne. They said his father was a god in ancient Egypt.

Daidalos, she thought, would probably be at work in a field higher up, where a ring of trees gave some measure of concealment. Glos would be with his sheep.

Thoughtfully she left the house, waved back the large and lazy cat, and climbed further. The skirl of a bagpipe came softly down the breeze; that would be the shepherd, playing from the pleasant shade of some tree. Tonight, by the fire, he would play for Inas and her father.

The path forked, the well-trod one leading to the right; the left which Inas followed rounded a rock and seemed to disappear into some thick brush. This she wriggled through. It was spiky and she came out, sucking a scratch on her wrist, into an open space— a shelving rock, narrowed to a peak and overlooking a long open meadow. Short grass grew here, and the place was ringed about by trees, which secretly shut it away from sight or sound of the world. At the further end a low hill rose behind an altar-shaped stone, almost repeating the rock on which Inas stood.

The trees here were both protection and a drawback. They shut out prying eyes, but they cut off the prevailing wind which was from the south. Today it blew freshly from the northwest.

Watching, she saw a strange thing. On the further rock which faced her at the length of the meadow, a curious, bird-like creature emerged. Its wings were longer than the wings of any bird, each twice the height of a man from tip to tip; its body more human than bird-like. The amazing creature advanced in short hops to the very edge of the little cliff, paused there a moment, then dived off and came sailing, gently tipping, to the meadow below, to glide, with long, wind-aided hops, down the grassy flat.

Inas raised her hands to her mouth and let out a long, hooting call, the call of the little brown owl. The winged creature turned as though to fly toward her but stopped with a bump.

"Oh, Father," Inas ran down the slope toward Daidalos. "How splendidly the new wings go. Now let me try them!"

Daidalos removed his arms from the glider and walked to meet her. "You are well, my child?" he asked absently.

This man, the greatest genius of his age and people, had the long head of the thinker, the square-tipped fingers of the craftsman. His graying hair was drawn back tightly and for convenience' sake twisted with a bone pin at the nape of the neck. His garb was simple: the high boots necessitated by the scrub and brush of Cretan hills, a kilt short and scant for the same reason, held by a wide belt with a dagger thrust in its side.

Here was a simple man, devoid of ostentation, scorning the usual palace politics and oratory, withdrawn from the world for the sake of what he might, in the end, contribute to it. For that, the world was suspicious, waiting to condemn openly, even to destroy.

Inas bent to pick up the strange, winged affair he had laid on the grass. It was light and strong, of carefully split bamboo tied with strong twine, the ends bent together to form rigid bird-like wings. The tail was flat, like a gull's tail, with a frame of cane, and like the wings surfaced with thin, strong linen cloth strapped down by light cords that crossed and recrossed the top.

"This is a new pattern, isn't it?" asked the girl. "And it seems heavier than the others. Does that matter?"

Her father shook his head. "It is new, but I cannot see that the increased weight is of much concern. Owing to the strong wind I have been unable to fly for two days." His words confirmed her guess. "I spent the time in making this and another, square, without the wing shaped tips. It seems to make curiously little difference whether the wings are square or pointed." His tone was puzzled. "Though I know no bird with square tipped wings."

As they walked back the length of the meadow, Inas told him of the landing of the fleet, and that Kadmos had brought her so far in the chariot. Together they climbed the rock from which Daidalos had flown. Behind this, in the hillside, there was a small dry cave, its entrance nearly hidden by a pile of brush. Here the gliders were stored when not in use.

Inas parted the branches and with her father's help brought out a winged affair of her own construction. This was as large as the other but lighter, and she had borrowed dyes and paints from the palace workshops to tint its wings. They were colored like those of some tropical bird, bright yellow at the body, shading out to flame-colored tail and wing-tips; and where her body would hang, between the arm holds, she had crudely sketched a bird's head. The proportions were strange, but from a little distance the effect might be startling, even unexpectedly terrifying.

Inas looked over the twine lashings and examined the bamboos closely for signs of weakness. That was Daidalos' command and the conditions under which she was allowed to play at this new and exciting sport. All was well. She stepped into the space between the two long bamboos and the wings and lifted the light framework off the ground. A breeze caught the underside, causing it to struggle with her as though it were a living creature, but at last she had her arms extended over the wings, wrists and shoulders through loops of sewn goatskin.

Now for a short run to get what speed she could so that when she jumped, the tail would clear the ledge! She drew back as far as the narrow space would let her, then, keeping the nose down, charged forward. One last leap and her feet were off the ground. She was in space, actually supported on the wings, for one long, ecstatic minute. Then her feet touched again.

She loved this sensation. For her there was none of the baffling disappointment felt by her father. Inas had no scientific problems to solve. With the wind behind her she advanced in giant steps down the long meadow and, approaching the limit, began to shorten her steps in preparation for a safe stop, lest she crash into the rock at the end. But by some quirk of the wind she lost her foothold and swung around, almost in a half circle, facing back to the way in which she had come. And surprisingly, with the wind against her, she was carried back, half the length of the field.

This was indeed strange and startling. Neither Inas nor Daidalos had considered that the wings, unlike the sails of a boat, might go better against the wind than with it. Unable quite to believe what had just happened, she swung back and scrambled to the top of the small ledge. There, against the wind, she adjusted the wings and slipped her arms into the straps as before, save that this time the wind would be against her.

Half hoping, she took off, her tongue between her teeth, her eyes dark with discovery. A long glide, far longer than any she had made before. The experiment had been a success.

Daidalos, who had been watching her with keen intentness, now came racing down the field to join her. "What did you do then?" he called sharply before he had reached her.

"Wasn't that wonderful, Father? The best flight we have made yet."

"Answer me," he commanded, his voice curt with impatience.

"It was the wind, I think," she explained. "When I stepped off like that—" she illustrated with the palms of her hands planing like the glider—"the wind seemed to hold me up . . . so . . . more strongly and more steadily than when it blew behind me. Wait, I'll do it again and you can see."

She ran back up the trail, struggling to hold the wings steady, then adjusted them a third time and took off. It was true. As before she seemed actually to ride the wind, sailing down in a long beautiful glide almost to her father's feet.

"You know," she cried, slipping out of the harness, "that a gull will ride the breeze like that. Oh, Father, I really believe we have found something, at last." Then, surprised at the expression on her father's face, she turned to follow his eyes to the entrance to the field.

A figure stood there, watching them. Short and stocky, clad in a nondescript garment tied on with tags and ends of rawhide, it waited in silence and without moving.

Inas glanced at her father's set face, then remembered that he was unable to recognize a figure so far off. She laughed reassuringly and scrambled to her feet.

"It is only Glos, Father. See, he comes toward us." She waved a bare brown arm in greeting to the keeper of Daidalos' flocks.

"Hail, Glos," she called gaily; and as he drew nearer, "Have you come then, at last, to try our wings?"

Daidalos' tense expression had relaxed and Inas, seeing his relief, felt a sudden clutch at her heart and glanced quickly away. This plan, not the intricacies of the world-famous Labyrinth, the king's store-house, not the wonders of the palace fountains, not the strong north citadel of the town, this alone was the darling of his heart. To fly, to give to the world a new freedom, to his people a new strength, a wonder such as man had never dreamed of, that was his desire. He knew, as Inas did, the dangers he incurred by these experiments. One prying courtier, a whisper in the ear of an enemy, and his plans, his whole career, perhaps his very life, would be forfeited. Not Minos himself could save him then.

Witchcraft! How could the people, common, ignorant, sunk in nearly twenty centuries of peace and ease, forgive a man who dared defy the laws of the gods and become a bird? When did men ever forgive one of themselves who dared to be different?

As she watched the approach of the shepherd all this flashed through her mind. He strode the length of the meadow, came nearer without a word. But Glos was always like that, taciturn, even without speech for days on end. They knew his loyalty and no words were needed.

When he stood close to them he still waited in silence till Daidalos motioned him to speak; then his voice came, rough as though from disuse, from behind the thick brown beard that covered the lower part of his face.

"There is talk," he said, "among the others who keep the sheep. Talk of a great bird that hovers over the fields of Daidalos, or of a new god, strange and with giant wings, such as none have beheld before."

He paused, scratched an ear and almost a smile seemed to flitter across his dour countenance. "And as all know, what is today talk of the shepherds, tomorrow will be held as truth by kings, and by the fools of the town."

Daidalos frowned. "I do not care." He seemed already to defy the world, as though it faced him there in the open field. "My wings are of too great value, my plans too important to be put aside for such silly sheep, blatting their terrors to each other." His mouth was stern, his eyes frowning and dark.

Inas spoke quickly. "But, Father, what does it matter?" Then she had a sudden idea. "Father, if this is true, if against the wind is better for our flight than with the wind, as we have been flying, then this field is not the best place for our plans. It has always been bad. See, you have had to wait three days for the south wind to veer to north. The hill is too high, and the breezes shifting and unstable. Look, I know a better place."

She put a pleading hand on his arm. "Out by the cliffs to the north of Knossos. Remember? There are caves there, deep and hidden. Kadmos and I used them for play houses long ago. And there is a flat grassy field below, before the cliff meets the sea, and the wind blows there steadily all day long."

Her father's gaze swung around, amused and understanding. Not unknowingly could he be coaxed to consider his own welfare, but if his plans were not interrupted—

"You are right," he agreed. "We can dismantle the wings and Glos shall take them, rolled together, by night, to the cliffs you speak of. Come." His decision was quickly made. "We will make them ready to move."

Glos nodded dour approval. "Good, then you will go tomorrow."

It was not a question but Daidalos chose to take it so. "Yes, we will go tomorrow."

Inas hoisted her glider upon her shoulder and started across the field. "I'll make them ready, Father," she called back. "Go, then, to the house with Glos and help with the evening meal. I shall be hungry when I return."

But in reality she wanted an excuse to be alone, to think out what could be done to ward off this increasing menace of discovery.

CHAPTER FIVE

THE CITY OF KNOSSOS

Inas loved the city of Knossos. From far off like this, sunset glowed on its painted house fronts, a bronze spear flashed winking like some mirrored signal from the lower walls of the palace as a sentry paced his steps. There was a muffled roar of distant voices; sound of work and play from a hundred thousand people rose like incense to the gods from the far-away streets of the town; and there was a new smell, not perhaps so good as the smell of country, but—Inas wrinkled her nose—she loved it, for it was Knossos, and her city.

Below them to the left flowed the little river of Kairatos with its wide, spreading banks. Straight ahead, sprawling over valley and hills, was the town. They crossed a viaduct along the hillside, then a stone bridge that spanned a tributary ravine, and finally came to a fork in the road.

One way led to the palace. This road was for the use of the

royal household, for ambassadors and captains and messengers to the king, and for traders and those who would do business with the thousand souls that lived within its wide-flung walls. The other fork led past a little blue-painted inn, where water splashed coolly in a fountain and small cooking fires already prepared the evening meal. Down this road Daidalos turned his mule.

They had been riding all afternoon; Daidalos mounted on a large black animal with a white nose, Inas perched far back, as was the Cretan manner, on a little white mule that she had named Ion, after the violets that bloomed around its home meadow. This had been no such exciting ride as behind the ponies Kadmos drove, and Inas had covered this stretch of road, from her father's country place to the city house, so often that it bore no surprises. She sighed a little wearily and thought how glad she would be to get bathed and put on fresh garments and once more eat a pleasant meal of Teeta's cooking.

At least it was a consolation to know that their gliders were safe. Rolled into four long tubular packages, bound with cord, they were now in the care of the shepherd. Inas' favorite glider had been left behind in the cave, just as it was, gay with paint and feathers. Another trip must be made to dismantle that. It had taken last evening and most of the morning to prepare the others, make them safe from prying eyes. Glos, somewhat reluctant to go, had definite orders to find the particular cave in the cliff which Inas had judged most safe for their plans. As soon as it was dark enough for safety, he would start for the north shore.

They came now to the lower reaches of the town. Here, on the narrow streets with scarcely room for the mules to pass between the crowding, close-packed houses, lived the poorer people, laborers, freed slaves, petty traders. The dwellings were of an older century, mostly three stories in height, the first and second

floors without windows. This was the construction of the earlier days when intertribal feuds made every man's house his own
small fort. The housetops were pleasantly irregular, each flat roof
throwing up a squarish, small-eyed watch-tower.

They mounted steadily, passed a market where, in the growing coolness, the merchants gathered to talk of the morning's
sales, where with thump and clack a weaver worked late at his
loom, and the mingled clash of cymbals and the beat of a drum
announced that a professional story-teller was about to begin his
tale. Dogs barked, children's voices rose shrill and clear on the
evening air and Inas nodded to left, smiled to the right, as neighbors greeted their return.

Now the mules climbed without guidance and turned through
a twisting street. Here the road widened and the houses were
larger, the house fronts gay with colored tiles, decorated with flying-fishes and bright processions, with sea-gulls, pheasants, and
blowing flowers in the painted grass. All were faded by sun and
sea air, mellowed into a pleasant soft tapestry that blended one
house with its neighbors. Here were wide windows on every
story, stairways that ascended from open courts, and everywhere
the plash of water, the cooling tinkle of many fountains.

The hoofs of Daidalos' mule clattered into his courtyard and
he threw the reins to a small slave boy who darted from one of
the low buildings. The man slid from his mount and, without
glancing behind, disappeared through a curtained doorway.

"Hail, Mufu!" greeted Inas and let herself slip from Ion's back.
The boy, grinning with a flash of white teeth, led the animals
away.

A small, long-furred black kitten scuttled crab-fashion across
the court and rubbed, with soft purrs of welcome, against Inas'
ankles; then evading her caressing hand, it scampered away into

the shadow on some game of its own. This was Sizi and the grandson, three generations removed, of the cat in the shepherd's hut. It seemed to have lost the ancestral dignity of its worshiped grandparents from Egypt.

Inas, laughing, made a futile dive after the kitten, then stretched mightily and having glanced around the windows of the courtyard, twirled into a cart-wheel to limber the stiffness from her muscles. One . . . two . . . three . . . across the small court. She landed lightly, upright and poised, hands over head, to start back again when a sharp *"Inas!"* came in scandalized tones from within the house.

Guiltily but with dancing eyes, the dimple full in evidence, Inas let her hands fall in mock dejection to her sides.

"Yes, Teeta!" she murmured demurely. Then taking the offensive: "Is the food prepared, Teeta? I am very hungry."

"Bathe first, then you may eat," commanded Teeta. She appeared in the curtained doorway, a small, slight woman, stockier than the slender Cretans, with a dark skin and full, wide mouth. Her kinky hair was quite gray and her eyes, deep set beneath wrinkled lids, glowed like black coals. She wore a long straight skirt of stiff blue linen, around her withered neck was a collar of flat blue stones and in her ears quivered square-cut lapis earrings. No flicker of expression crossed her leathern countenance, but Inas knew her old nurse was glad of her return. She who had been nurse also to Daidalos was completely unimpressed by the recognized genius of her master or by the skill of his small daughter.

Now she followed Inas to the bath and lighted three little lamps, wicks floating in pottery bowls of oil. Hot water, fine sponges, and scented powders were there, and wood ashes with a flask of warmed olive oil. She took away the girl's high boots and dust-stained garments and brought others, chattering all the while.

"This trip of yours, it was all nonsense. With the bull-vaulting but three days off you should be at the palace, not playing about the country. If it had happened that your mule had fallen with you—" she scolded. "How are Nasos and my sister? No matter. If they had not been well you would have told me."

Inas chuckled. "Kadmos is back." She spoke through the steam that filled the small room and poured olive oil to mingle with fine wood ashes into her hand. This, rubbed on the body, formed a pleasant and cleansing emulsion.

"Kadmos? Do you think I am deaf as well as blind? The boy has been here twice today, as though that would hasten your return. And twice yesterday. There is a gift for you also . . . No, wait till you have finished with your bath . . . And the Princess Ariadne has sent for you . . . you are to see her in the morning."

Still chattering, the old woman departed to tend her master's needs and hasten the evening meal. Inas lolled back in the tub, splashing the water happily with wet brown palms.

Around the wall one octopus linked arms with another in rhythmic harmony, symbol of the Cretan Empire. They reminded her of Kadmos and his father's boat, and of Kadmos' mysterious gift that awaited her somewhere in the house. Curiosity returned. The pleasant smell of roasting fish wafted from the open court-yard kitchen reminded her also that it was many hours since her last meal. She scrambled from the tub and rubbed herself dry, then donned the garments Teeta had left for her.

On her bare feet she slipped soft sandals of embroidered yellow kidskin, then slipped into a dress of yellow linen, its skirt half trousers, frilled at the hem, each tiny ruffle edged with a fringe of deeper color. The waist of darker hue was very tight at the belt, for all Cretans, both men and women, were vain of their small waists; its slimness was almost a mark of their nationality. The neck was slashed to the waist in front, and opened over a thin chemise of fine white linen.

The steam of the bath had curled her shimmering hair into a hundred tiny ringlets. Now with a comb of ivory she divided it into five long curls, three at the back, one before each ear, and the front, clipped to a short fringe, was screwed and patted with the palm of her hand into a dozen small flat curls across the forehead.

Inas wiped the steam from the bronze mirror and bent forward to examine her small, scrubbed face. Yes, the hair would do. A daffodil-hued ribbon above the fringe held the curls in place. Now a touch of red ochre for the cheeks? No, best not, though Ariadne used it to perfection, together with kohl about her dark eyes. But Daidalos thought his daughter too young for such vanities. Inas sighed, patted disapprovingly at the dimple-like scar on her cheek. She hated that scar, though she had won it in fair sport with a huge black bull when she was only ten. She glanced once more at her reflection, then pulled aside the curtain of the bath and called:

"Teeta, I come!" warningly. The gods be kind to Teeta if the flavor of that fish were not half so delicious as its smell!

CHAPTER SIX

THE PRINCESS ARIADNE

Inas wove her way through the narrow upper streets that led to the palace. Only two more days till the bull-vaulting. Inas found she could make her heart drop, then soar wildly, whenever she thought of it. It was all very wonderful . . . but a little frightening too. Never before had she been in the great arena, with thousands of eyes upon her, thousands of throats to shout praise or blame if she won—or lost.

Daidalos had been reassuring when he told her that after the very first you were never aware of the vast audience above; you just went right ahead, as though you were alone with the bull in an open field. And Daidalos should know. No one of his generation had been more skillful in the ring. Part of his present unpopularity was due to his having given up the sport while he was still strong and active. He had stated, with amazing honesty but extreme lack of tact, that he was wasted in the Bull Ring, that his mind could do more for his people than by inventing acrobatics to amuse them.

He had made much needed improvements in the arena, designed some generations before by his great-grandfather, another Daidalos, and for a time his popularity had returned. He had improved Knossos itself with his engineering projects and had placed fountains of running water in every open court of the city. All these were very fine, grumbled the populace, but they still missed their favorite bull-vaulter.

Then he had put forward a scheme for the defense of the palace, plans for a fortress such as Crete had never known.

This unfortunately meant additional taxes and labor for the population. It was in vain that Daidalos pointed out the growing power of many cities in northern Africa, the increasing jealousy of Crete's own settlements along the southern coast of the Ægean and on the islands to the north. Crete, according to her people, had always been fortified by her ships, her wooden walls. Her sea-power was supreme, had been for a thousand years and for unknown time before that. No other defense was necessary.

After considerable argument Daidalos managed to fortify the north gate to the palace. Minos himself was against further effort in that line—for what king will admit that his power is waning, that his strength is not as great as ever? The famous engineer, disgusted, turned his attention to plans of his own. This flying idea had always been close to his heart. Now he had leisure and, by living in great simplicity, enough money to work on it, if some fool of the court didn't take it into his head to further that "witchcraft" tale!

Inas frowned absently at a group of strangers, traders from the south, who were apparently discussing her unusual hair, nodded and smiled at an upper window where she recognized two girls over an embroidery frame, and turned back her thoughts to considerations of her father's problem. She knew that Daidalos incurred great danger by his present experiments. If the gods had intended man to fly, they would have created him with wings, like the birds. That, she knew, would be the opinion of other Cretans. But she herself found it almost impossible to consider the flying as other than a delightful new sport. She believed that if every man could try the wings that Daidalos had constructed, could feel the rush of air beneath his feet, the delicious moment of supremacy over a new element, so akin, yet so different, from man's power beneath the water, then each would for himself become converted to this new idea. But to condemn it just because it was *new* . . .

Inas dodged a train of donkeys toiling toward the palace with panniers of pineapples from the Fleet. She crowded close into a doorway while they passed, then darted out and rounded a corner. Here wide shallow steps rose toward the palace road, a short cut denied the laden donkeys.

Though it was early, the upper road already swarmed with people; laborers, lesser craftsmen who worked within the walls but dwelt with their families in the lower town, traders with their wares, men who sought business or judgment from the king, or interviews with his courtiers. The girl was known to many and received greetings from right and left. In two more days all would know her—for success or failure. Would Kadmos keep his promise and attend the Bull Ring? She must send him one of the purple-dyed shells that would admit him to the lower tiers of seats. Also she must return the pin he had lent her.

Smiling, she touched her hair, now twined at the back and fastened with a new pin of crystal and gold. That had been the mysterious gift of last evening; this he had brought to replace the one she had lost in diving from the sponge boat.

The palace was vast, with long echoing corridors of bright painted stone, with pillars of the characteristic shape, wide at the top, narrowing to the rounded base, that marched in endless files, supporting the great hewed and painted beams. Stairways led away to upper stories and half-stories, since the building sprawled over a half-dozen different levels on the hillside, and one glimpsed cool, shaded courts where vines and roses grew, terraces and light-wells; windowless inner rooms open to the sky but shaded from the hot glare of the sun. This was the palace proper, where only those connected with the royal family might penetrate.

The girl ran up low shallow stairs to the second floor, along a pillared hallway hung with curtains of purple embroidered in gold, and came out on an open terrace. Here, in the shade overlooking the town and the road to the hills, was the favorite retreat of the Princess Ariadne. Voices and laughter had guided Inas to this airy retreat.

Ariadne lounged on a long, cushioned couch. Inas paused in the doorway, facing her. The princess must have come recently from some ceremony as priestess of the palace temple, for she still wore the ceremonial leopard skin apron over her full, flounced dress with its long divided skirt. Her dark hair was in the five formal ringlets, the small curls on the forehead held in place by a gold fillet that bound her brows. Her face was gay, impudent, even reckless, with a pert little tip-tilted nose and a red mouth that turned up sharply at the corners. Her dark eyes, rimmed with kohl, were full of mischief. A lovely, lovable princess, this Ariadne of Crete.

A LOVELY, LOVABLE PRINCESS,
THIS ARIADNE OF CRETE

At sight of Inas she leaped to her feet and crossed the terrace to slip an affectionate arm about the waist of the girl.

"My child, you have been long away. We have missed you here in the court."

She waved a gaily encompassing hand around the terrace where women worked at tapestry frames, carded fine wool, or sat on cushions about a small blue monkey, Ariadne's African pet. Some of the women looked up, two or three smiled, and would have come forward to talk to her, but the princess had the prior claim.

Now she drew Inas aside to a shallow flight of steps, cushioned with bright colors, which mounted against the blank wall of the palace, a pleasant seat. She pulled the daughter of Daidalos down beside her and began to chatter of palace gossip. Had Inas seen the costumes for the bull-vaulting? Someone had brought her a small dog from Egypt: one of the slaves was washing it now. There was a new fruit which Meropes had sent her, plucked at some island port where the Fleet had put in.

Inas listened and nodded, amused. Was this the reason Ariadne had sent for her to come to the palace, this empty, girlish chatter of the princess's maidens?

Then Ariadne made a swift and unexpected change of subject. "The tribute of Greek slaves is here."

This was indeed surprising. What could be a princess's concern with these unfortunate captives from the north?

"Yes, they came before I left Knossos," Inas said; then, startled at Ariadne's expression, she followed the direction of the other's gaze. Far below them wound the road to the hills, the road from the sea. Along that road must have marched the Greeks after landing at the mouth of the Kairatos. "Have you seen them?" she asked the princess.

Ariadne dropped her eyes and played with the tassel on a cushion beside her. After a moment she answered, scarcely above a murmur. "Yes . . . I have seen them." Then, "You speak their language, Inas?"

"Greek? Yes, I speak it. Father had it taught me when I was young."

"Then go—" Ariadne laid a gentle hand on Inas arm—"go to the Greeks and see if all is well with them. See if they are fed and are kindly treated and if they have all that they need. They are in the Labyrinth, below the council chamber."

That a princess should consider the possible health of a dozen or so Greek slaves, barbarians, dirty probably, and uncouth, from some strange land across the sea, mere tribute of her father's might! Inas was astonished.

"Here—" the princess glanced around, saw that none of the women were observing them—"I will give you my ring, that you may pass the guards. This will take you anywhere, grant you anything that you need." Ariadne drew from her finger an oval gold seal deeply cut with her insignia of a priestess and a small deer. Inas took it slowly, slipped it on her pointed finger, and sat twisting it admiringly as Ariadne told her tale.

The slaves had come along that road from the north. It was late in the afternoon, just ten days ago—the princess seemed to have kept admirable count of the time—and there had been . . . she spoke haltingly . . . one among them, tall and with hair of a strange light brown in curls about his wide brow. He walked proudly, a prince among men, "towering above the Cretan guards as a pine towers above the laurels of the hillside."

Inas' eyes were grave with interest. "And you wish word of this man, Princess."

"Oh!" Ariadne hastened to assure her, "news of them all. Poor

creatures, alone and fearful, in a strange land and with none to
speak their language!"

Inas suppressed her inclination to remind the other that many
of the palace slaves were Greek, perhaps even the palace guards,
and that, without doubt, many could speak to them in their own
tongue. But the princess continued:

"Yes, and news of him also, if you wish. His name is Thes . . .
Theseus." Her tongue stumbled on the unfamiliar word. "And
without doubt he is the son of a king and unaccustomed to the
crude fare of prisoners."

"I had never heard that the Greeks were so greatly softened to
the luxuries of life," commented Inas, "but I will go. For the sake
of yourself, and for my mother's sake, who was one of them."
And perhaps a little for her own curiosity, she thought to herself. "Make an errand for me," she told the princess. "Say that I
have gone to fetch—" her eyes roved the terrace—"a skein of colored yarn that you may match your latest shuttle for the weaving.
I will bring it when I come and so put a stop to any gossip."

"Good." Ariadne patted her hand, then gave her a little push
toward the doorway. "But hasten!"

Inas sped down the corridor toward the stair. A fresh sea wind
smelling pleasantly of far places rippled the curtains along the
hall, and as always there was the soft sound of running water,
tinkling, purling, gurgling its underground way through the
vast building. Kadmos had once told her that no other city in the
world had so many fountains, so much running water as Knossos. It was a gay sound, a delightful accompaniment to the murmuring life of the palace. A slave passed her, bearing a basket
heaped with fragrant violets, plucked just this morning on the
slopes of the mountain.

Below stairs were the offices of the king, his council chamber and throne room, with its royal decorations of the fleur-de-lis, and its snarling griffins crouching on the painted wall behind the simple stone seat that was the ancient throne of all Cretan kings. Here Minos sat to dispense justice and to receive his ministers and ambassadors. Inas, passing down the hall of pillars, glimpsed the guardsmen on duty, each with the great bronze double-headed ax of the king's body-guard. She saw that the captains of the Fleet were in council with Minos and recognized Meropes among the group.

Perhaps it was her haste to complete her errand and return to Ariadne; perhaps she was too intent on seeing if Kadmos might be present in the council chamber; or possibly the tall Egyptian always walked with so stealthy a tread. But a few steps beyond the door of the throne room Inas, with her head still turned back over her shoulder, felt a soft touch on her arm. She whirled, startled, to meet the gaze of Kres.

She murmured an embarrassed greeting and paused to face this narrow-chested man, master of the gold workers and one of the greatest men in all Crete.

He acknowledged her greeting with a curt inclination of his lean bald head. Inas bit her lip and reddened with mingled amusement and exasperation. Kres might be a wise man and a brilliant one, but he was also crafty, mean, avaricious, and as in-quisitive as a cat.

Now he held her, for a moment, in brief conversation. Was she well! And her father? Yes?

Puzzled, because Kres could have no interest in the welfare of her household, Inas still sought to escape, to hasten on her errand, then caught his sharp eyes examining her hand. Involun-tarily she folded her thumb over Ariadne's ring. But Kres might have caught an earlier glimpse of it, might even have forced the encounter for the sake of his curiosity.

She would not satisfy that! Besides, the secret was not her own. Hastily she excused herself—"A message to deliver . . . yarn from the store-room"—and hurried away. But she felt the questioning mean little eyes of the gold worker boring through her spine, all the way down the corridor.

Another flight of stairs, these steeper and longer, took her into a cool, earthy-smelling passage. This was small and narrow, lighted solely by a shaft from some upper court. It seemed only a blind alley till the end was reached, when it opened out into another of the same shape and beyond that into still another. At each corner and turning point was posted a black guard with the double ax of Minos. Inas found it scarcely necessary to show her ring, for all knew her and guessed her to be on some commission for the princess.

At the far eastern end of the Labyrinth, the Hall of the Labrys, named for its decorative frieze of row on row of the royal double ax, were the store-rooms; beyond those were dungeons reserved for political prisoners; then the cells stored with oils and with wine and gold and other treasures from Crete's tributary kingdoms; then came other rooms where were stored tablets with the royal accounts; and finally a group of small chambers. Here, as of old, were the Greeks. Inas remembered that Teeta had told her of her own mother's imprisonment in these very rooms.

The door was barred, but the guard swung it open for her and she found herself in a low square chamber, not small, newly washed with lime so that every bit of sunlight from above glanced back from the clean bright walls. The floor was spread with mats and beyond was a paved bathing place with a small stone trough of running water. In this room were the seven maidens; the youths were further along the corridor.

Pausing in the doorway Inas glanced around. For a moment she felt breathless, almost frightened as though she had blundered into a nest of shy, wild animals. Then she thought, "Poor things, to be so terrified! Why can't they guess we'll be kind to them!"

"Greetings, hail to you from the north!" she stammered in their own tongue.

No one spoke or moved. The girls crouched or knelt, silently impassive, on the mats. They had been given food, water, and fresh clothes after their long sea voyage but had apparently refused the strange Cretan garb, preferring their own simple unsewn chitons and shawls.

After a moment a small bundle huddled in a corner stirred slightly and one bright, pansy-brown eye peered from the folds of a ragged gray shawl.

Inas saw a flicker of interest in that glance and crossed the room. For a moment she felt almost a shiver of fear go up her spine. It was a little like entering a den of mountain leopards, so great was the fear and hatred concentrated in that small place. But the feeling passed and she half knelt on the mat beside the small, bright-eyed bundle and without touching it, asked, "What is your name?"

The eye regarded her unblinking.

Inas smiled. "Don't be afraid," she said earnestly. "Please tell me your name, for I want to make friends."

The shawl was lowered an inch, disclosing the other eye. "Dité," murmured a small voice.

"Dité? My mother's name was Aphrodite, after the goddess of the Greeks."

"Your mother?" The shawl slipped a trifle further.

"She also was a Greek."

"Oh, then you are a slave."

"No." Inas made herself more comfortable beside the other. She felt that every ear in the room was listening. But perhaps this was the best road toward reassurance. "I am no slave. I am free, and of a free father, as you too may be free someday."

"Freedom is not for us." Dité let the shawl fall to her knees, disclosing a small, heart-shaped face, eyes red-rimmed with weeping, a mouth made for laughter but now twisted to hold back the tears. "No, in two days' time we are to be fed to that horrible monster, the Minotaur."

"Nonsense!" Inas spoke sharply. "There is no Minotaur. That is a tale for children, like those tales about the web-fingered green sea-gnomes, who can change their shape and control the weather."

"Oh . . . Oh . . . !" Dité's small mouth was a circle of amazement. "But indeed they are real! Men have seen them." She put her hand on Inas' knee for emphasis and the Cretan girl noted how fine and soft it was. This was no common little shepherd girl.

"Yes?" Inas pretended amazement. "But the Minotaur is *not* true. Wait, do not weep, and you shall see. He is just a white bull, or a black one, like any other your father must have kept among his cattle. Only that he is put in the ring, with crowds of people watching, and we who are accustomed to such sport, play with him, and let him chase us."

"Ah, but you will be armed, and protected by shields, and by men with swords."

"No. *No*, I tell you. We go in alone, and unarmed. O Britomartis, show me the way to convince this child." Unconsciously she had dropped into her own tongue, then at the startled gasp that ran round the room, recovered herself. "You are comfortable here?" she asked. "The food is good? There is nothing I can send you?"

"The food is good, though strange." A neighboring girl, somewhat older than Dité, spoke for them all. "If we are to be saved only to make a feast for the Minotaur, what does it matter? But we should like some goats' milk, if possible."

"That shall be sent you," promised Inas. "Now do not fear. For a few days you will wait here, two or three more, perhaps. Then if you are all well, if no disease has developed, there will be a sale. The king allows only his friends to purchase a Greek; it is a great honor. My own mother was a Greek," she spoke now to the whole room. "The men, after they have been tested in the Bull Ring, also will be sold, or given, to members of the court. Now I must go."

She felt their eyes on her as she rose and crossed to the doorway, felt that she had gained a little of their confidence—but not much. Turning, she smiled reassuringly at Dité and received in return a tremulous quiver of the small mouth.

CHAPTER SEVEN

THESEUS

Beyond the room of the Greek girls was another, smaller, not so well lighted, but still clean, and freshly lime-washed. Here, behind the barred door guarded by two armed Cretan guards, were the male slaves.

Inas displayed her ring, and the guard with the double-headed ax lowered his weapon in salute to this symbol of royalty, then grinned in friendly, unofficial fashion and waved her toward the barred door.

"It's safe enough, I think. But better stay close to the doorway," he cautioned her. "Those fellows hate anyone who wears the look of an honest Cretan. Brr—" He shuddered in a terror that was not all mockery. "One of them, the tall one with the mat of hair, nearly strangled old Esos here." He nodded toward his companion.

"That's true." Esos rubbed his grizzled throat in rueful reminiscence. He was an old campaigner, too old now for active warfare; he remembered, he said, when they used to fight those fellows on their own stony beaches. "Good soldiers too," he approved as one veteran to another. "But tricky, sly as foxes. We beat them, and in fair battle. That's why they have to send this tribute every ten years, seven youths and seven maidens, the best they can pick."

"Yes, yes, we know." The other guard interrupted the well-worn tale. "But watch the tall one, he's not to be trusted," he reminded the girl.

Close inside the doorway was a trencher of food; fruit and meat and big slabs of unleavened bread. Pressing close to the bars, Inas saw that they had not yet been locked again. She pushed aside the barrier and entered.

The cell was small and, like the girls' room, smelled strangely. As the smell of a dog differs from that of a cat, so does the odor of one race differ from that of another. Three of the group sat crouched together, talking, in one corner of the room. They fell silent, scowling blackly at the intruder. One slept, sprawled upon the bare floor; great, sun-browned limbs outflung in complete relaxation. Two others played a game with their fingers, counting and guessing. The seventh stood alone, uncompromisingly, against the wall, and instantly Inas recognized the princess's description. Here indeed was the pine that towered above the laurel.

He was far taller than the men of the slender, small-boned Cretan race. Inas' Greek blood gave her the advantage of an inch or two over most men of her own country. Theseus' mop of untidy hair, leaf brown, fell to his shoulders, again a contrast to the usual formal arrangement of Cretan locks. Heavy brows met over a straight, thick-bridged nose with scornful curling nostrils, wide deep-set gray eyes formed his best feature, and a heavy full-lipped mouth dipped arrogantly at the corners. Huge shoulders, wrists like bars of brass, hands that could crush the life from a man's throat in one convulsive grip.

Inas gazed at him a moment through concealing lashes. Yes, the creature might be attractive . . . if you liked that kind. Ariadne had perhaps seen too many men of the court, effete, a little precious. She should live for a time with the divers of the sponge fleet, eat bread and cheese with the shepherds on the hills, then she would value this hulking mass of bone and muscle at its true worth.

The silence continued. Inas' mind raced like a very small mouse in a closed little trap. How to pierce through this awkward stillness, deliver her message and be gone? Theseus stood unmoving, his arms folded across his chest.

Inas gulped. "Greetings!" she murmured, in repetition of her former salutation.

No one spoke, but the "pine" bowed its matted head.

"I bring a message from Minos' daughter, the Princess Ariadne." She spoke directly to the leader, obviously Theseus.

"There is no message Minos' daughter could send us that we should care to hear," affirmed the Greek. His accent was strange to Inas, but she followed it with little difficulty.

"No matter. I have been sent. Greetings from the princess and good wishes for your health. Your women have asked for goats' milk. Can I obtain food that you also might desire? There is a market here—" Inas nodded toward the town—"with foods from many ports. Perhaps our fruits are strange and unpalatable to your tongues?"

There was a growl of assent from the corner, but Theseus frowned and the mutter subsided. "We have no complaint," he stated firmly. "Go back and tell your mistress— You are a slave?" And as Inas shook her head, "Tell her that we have all we need. We have come in payment of a debt, like honorable soldiers, and pay it we shall, and without complaint."

Then his gaze wandered to the wall behind her. Inas shrugged. No matter. "If you have any needs, tell the guards and they will send for me. The gods be with you." She stepped out into the corridor, closing the bars behind her.

"You had success?" asked the man with the double ax.

Inas shook her head. "Not much," she told him, but added the promise she had given Theseus. "It is the princess's orders." And having again displayed her ring to emphasize her words, she hurried down the hall.

Her next mission was to the dyers for the required yarn, that the women of Ariadne's train might not conjecture on her errand. They had, Inas thought, little else to do but gossip, shut up there together day after day, seeing the same faces, circling through a treadmill round of the same tasks. She did not blame them for their silly chatter, but one must protect the good name of the princess.

After that she must return to the town for her clothes, since the next few days would be spent in the palace and the Bull Ring. Or should she send a messenger? She considered, then decided that it would be better to return to Daidalos. He would want to see her, give her perhaps some last, wise counsel before the games.

She procured the yarn, hurried back to the terrace where the princess waited impatiently, and, under cover of discussing the color of the wool, Inas told Ariadne of her success, or lack of it, with the Greeks.

"There is a little one, Dité, among the girls," Inas continued, watching the princess's face. "I wish she might be under your protection."

"Perhaps you would like her for a gift," suggested Ariadne absently. "Your father—"

But Inas shook her head. "Father will have no more Greeks since Mother died. He had me taught the tongue, but he will not hear it spoken in the household. Perhaps you—"

"Theseus," murmured the princess dreamily. "It has a pleasant sound to the ear."

"His name is more pleasant than his manners," commented Inas; then quickly, "What think you of this hue? Is it too strong?"

Ariadne quickly raised the yarn to the light, then turned to the girl who had come up behind them. "Hana, we dispute. Be thou our judge. Is this color of sufficient strength? The last from the workshops was of too pale a tinge."

So went the afternoon. It was not until Inas was on the road toward home that she remembered Ariadne's ring, still upon her finger. Turning it she thought, "I must remember to give that back to her this very evening."

But many moons had gone and many ships had sailed, never to return, before the little gold seal with its priestess and its dancing deer was again on the finger of a Cretan princess.

CHAPTER EIGHT

THE BULL RING

In spite of the constant drumming in the distant town and the calls and shouts that rose in a murmuring wave even to the palace walls, the inner chamber where the ten girls slept, opening on the light-well, was pleasantly restful. Inas awoke as on any other morning and yawning drowsily would have turned over to sleep again. The light was still pale. Dawn was coming.

Sleepily she glanced down at her finger. Oh, Ariadne's ring! She had forgotten it after all, left it at home when, to avoid Teeta's curious glance, she had removed it the night before.

Then she heard whispers. Today . . . she raised herself on one elbow . . . today was the day of the bull-vaulting.

She pushed her bright hair away from her forehead and sat up. Hana and Aias were whispering and giggling together. The others still slept or lay quiet. Inas tossed back her covering and as she rose from the mat a conch-shell blew softly, then more impera-tively in the corridor. Time to arise. Already the increasing light proclaimed that night had departed.

An old slave woman brought them hot water to drink and fruit to eat, since no more solid food was allowed before they entered the Bull Ring. Then the girls, still sleepy, shivering in the early chill, were herded into the bath chamber, where after hot spong-ings, cold water was splashed on them by slave girls, and a vigor-ous rubdown with olive oil left them awake and fresh.

A short kilt of bright yellow, striped with green and black, was the costume for the acrobatic games, and completed by soft san-dals of hide bound with thongs about the ankles. The gold brace-lets and chains, always worn as a sign of gentle birth, were today laid aside lest a chain catch on a horn or a bracelet hinder the quick grip and prove dangerous in the ring. Inas' bright hair was bound back with a ribbon of flaming red and hung in five curls to her waist.

Aias, little and dark, strong as a hill donkey, paused in bind-ing her curls with a band of bright leaf green. "Perhaps I shall not need this tomorrow," she suggested half in jest. "I would it could be replaced by the gold wreath Kres has made."

All knew that wreath and coveted it. For ten years and more it had been among the palace treasures, a delicate tracery of sea tendrils and water grasses twined to form a crown, an award for some great feat of strength or bravery in the games. Even today, it might be awarded. Tonight even . . . Inas sighed. There was dan-ger, also, before them. Tonight they might not all be here.

Hana caught her hand, pressing it beneath her pounding heart. "Feel how it beats with excitement," she whispered, her eyes big and dark.

"Think not of your silly heart, foolish one!" Inas scolded her.

"Think of the geranium blooms in your garden, the fish we shall catch from Kadmos' blue-painted boat, the feast of tomorrow night. But think not of the bulls."

"That is wise counsel," the old slave woman told them gravely. "Foolish to vault the bull a hundred times, and ninety-nine of them merely in thought. Here are the wreaths."

For the procession into the ring each girl was given a fresh-twined crown of bright roses. Truly a gay procession they would make! Kilts of bright embroidered cloth, each weighted with a heavy fringe of gold, were adjusted over the underskirts. These would later be removed for greater freedom in the ring.

Then the conch-shell blew again. There was a last-minute scramble to settle wreaths on curling locks, pat fringes into place, jostle into proper position in the line. Down the long stone corridor, still chilly from the night wind, along the echoing halls, past the guard at the outer door, and then into early pale sunlight.

Inas drew a deep breath to quiet her heart which, like that of Aias, was hammering with excitement. She must steady it by turning her thoughts away from the coming events. The sun would be much higher before any of their number might be called. First there would be the procession, with sacrifice to Rhea (the mother) and to Britomartis (the sweet maiden), then the mock battles. Desperately she twisted her thoughts into calmer channels: the wings that reposed safely in the cavern above the cliffs, Kadmos' ponies and her swift ride behind them, the sum her sponges might have brought in the market—all pleasant familiar things—Sizi and his funny little pink-tipped nose, Ariadne's blue monkey . . .

Through the gate of the palace into full sunlight, and like a giant wave, breath-taking, engulfing, rose the roar from the crowd below, the audience already assembled in the arena.

The procession paused, to wait a moment on the wide steps that led to the river path. Here the boys joined them, gay in their brief embroidered kilts of plain yellow, their hair loose in ringlets similar to the girls', but without the curled fringe across the forehead. Each carried a tall rhyton of gold, a pointed cone-shaped cup holding oil for the sacrifice to Rhea and to her sister goddess, Britomartis.

Still another short pause, then the princess came to lead them. As daughter of Minos, who was high priest as well as king, she was leader of the priestesses and wore now the sacred knot, the tall crown of bright blue feathers with its high tasseled center, the leopard skin apron and full divided skirts of her station. In her hand was the incense sprinkler, her badge of office. Behind her walked two older priestesses carrying the cups with wine for the altar.

Inas' trained eye caught sight of these cups and she gasped with delight. The famous Bull Cups, the greatest pride of Minos' treasury. They also had been made by Kres, modeled so delicately and finely that every detail of the sculptured scenes on their golden sides, the tiny net which was thrown to catch the little raging bulls, the straining muscles of the men who pulled taut the ropes, the blades of trampled grass about the small carved hoofs, each last detail was like life itself reduced to a smallness beyond imagining. Someday she must beg Ariadne to let her examine them closely.

The conch-shell blew once more and the shifting nervous group settled into place. Slowly, with Ariadne in its lead, the procession stepped down the stone causeway.

Step by step, to the clash of cymbals, to the solemn roll of drums, they wound down the bank toward the river bed. Below them the roar increased, ten thousand voices raised in wild acclaim, almost drowning the sound of the music of their march.

Inas, without moving her head, swung her eyes to the right and looked down. Below her lay the Bull Ring, below and beyond that spread the fairgrounds, booths with their bright awnings fluttering in the sunny air; shelters that hid from the rising sun all manner of wares for sale, sweets and fruits in rough little stalls, the gold- and silversmiths' section with its special guard against foreign thieves, the booths where freshly killed meat was displayed, and beyond even those the bright sparkle of the little river.

As they dropped over the slope, almost directly beneath them was the great oval of the circus, outlined on one side by the awnings of indigo-dyed cloth that shaded the lower tiers of seats. A covering of royal purple indicated the boxes Minos and the princess would occupy and the freshly watered center ring sending up a pleasant smell of earth. At several places the bright shifting patchwork indicated the entrances, now jammed with tardy arrivals.

The gateway for the procession was kept for that alone. Already the drummers were announcing their coming! Inas felt a thrill of excitement. All this, and she was to be one of the main attractions! Then she felt a rising bubble of laughter as she seemed to hear Kadmos' voice in her ear, "Don't be so full of your own importance, my girl!"

Behind her Aias murmured, "What is the jest?" But Inas did not dare answer. Almost immediately a feeling of the solemnity of the occasion and the beauty of the bright pageant drowned the other impulse. And then they were at the gate, the special palace gate to the arena.

Here the way was sprinkled with flowers, with laurel and with roses, and the air was odorous of crushed geranium and orange petals. New mats had been laid to cover the dust and the sun brought out a pleasant smell of straw, clean and sharp. From beyond the further barrier came the sound of muffled bellowing. Those would be the bulls for the ring!

On either side of the gate ranged the palace guards, their faces like carvings beneath the gay, conical, tasseled caps, their uniforms bright with gold embroideries and their double axes glittering in the sunlight. Black, immovable as men of stone, they waited while the procession slowly filed into the inclosure. Inas ached to turn her head, to see every bit of this colorful, shouting, shifting pageant.

Color, color everywhere! The oblong inclosure itself was of plaster, tinted to a soft henna, and the lower tiers were cushioned with bright blue beneath the awning of indigo striped with white. The royal boxes were hung with tapestries and garlanded with strings of flowers and the green of the sacred ivy. The inner inclosure, the ring itself, was below the level of the first tier, with three entrances, one for the performers, one for the animals, and a third beneath the royal box, where the oval bent inward toward the altar to the goddesses. Here, after the games, the sacred animals would be led to sacrifice.

The procession entered the arena and formed on both sides of the altar, Ariadne in the center, fronting it. The roar of sound from the thousands who crowded the seats died to a hushed murmur. Inas tried to remember what a small, insignificant, almost unnoticeable part of this she was, but her knees were strangely unsteady and she wished she could sit down for a moment. Then the trumpets sounded outside the gateway and she forgot her momentary panic.

Minos was entering the arena. A wizened, yellow little man garbed in great splendor of high feathered and tasseled crown and jewel-incrusted robes, he paced slowly forward between his two sons. Inas knew that he had been brought from the palace in the royal palanquin with its gold-shot curtains, its high, feathered canopy, its cushions soft with down.

The audience rose, shouting as one man. Minos was beloved, but the plaudits were for Deukalion, the laughing prince. Straight and tall, with a waist of aristocratic slimness, jeweled and lithe beneath his crown of bright feathers, he raised his hand in salute to the multitude, smiled boyishly, then turned to the serious business before him.

The ceremonies that followed were picturesque, though wearying. Inas had seen them a hundred times before, though in lesser form. The invocation to Rhea, mother of all gods, guardian of trees and serpents, rocks and earth and the fertility of the soil. There was Ariadne's skillful whirling dance, the small golden double axes flashing in her hands, the pouring of wine from the Bull Cups, and the lighting of the flame on the altar between the two tall pillars. As the smoke and incense rose in a white cloud the multitude stood once more, and the oil was poured in libation to bring success, prosperity, fertility to their country. The flames died down. The boys with their golden rhytons, empty now, drew back and a little white heifer, hung with garlands, was slain before the altar, slain by Minos with one forceful, accurate stab of the bronze and ivory knife.

"O Rhea take thou this offering!" cried Minos, cried Ariadne and the priests, cried the voices from ten thousand throats. Then, the blood spilled on the altar, the body was dragged away by two white mules. The ground was sprinkled with water, swept with brooms of boughs, and the ceremonies were finished.

Above the oval inclosure four tall boxes waited for the novices; they were hung with curtains of dark red which shielded them from both spectators and sunlight. Ariadne sat with the girls; her younger brother, Anax, with the boy novices.

The first act of the circus was a mock battle between unhelmeted soldiers armed with long spears and men with small circular shields thickly padded with straw, leather covered. The spears were light and sharp. The game was to catch the blow of an opponent upon the shield; a sport of speed and agility. The crowd loved it and many wagers were laid on either side.

Inas watched for a time, then turned her attention toward the tiers of seats that rose against the sky. Through an opening in the curtains she could see without being seen and could gaze as she pleased without loss of dignity.

Daidalos would not be here, she knew. Probably he was now miles away on the cliffs with his glider, or experimenting in one of his various laboratories with one of his many interests—chemicals and herbs, water supply and drainage, the construction of boats. Anything seemed to interest an agile brain such as his; nothing was so perfect that he could not find some detail capable of improvement. The arena in its present form was his own construction, built by his direction. So Inas understood his absence from the bull-vaulting—that was over, complete and finished, something among his past interests, not his present concern.

But Kadmos, where was he? Her eyes examined the crowd. He might be anywhere, hidden in that enormous shifting throng. A shout arose and Inas turned back to the arena. Two spearmen had lost their spears, now quivering harmlessly, impaled in the straw of the shields. A point gained by the wielders of the shields.

An expert on footwork like all bull-vaulters, Inas concentrated for a moment on the spearman's stance and lunge. There! The point was caught again on the shield and plucked out only just in time to avoid a dexterous twist of the shield-wielder, which aimed to snap the spear shaft or wrest it from the owner's hand. But Inas had foreseen the two swift movements from the footwork which preceded them. True daughter of Daidalos, her active mind sought the flaw in that attack. "Thus and thus . . ." her toes and fingers clasped in accompaniment to her thoughts. "Thus and thus—weaving the body . . . *ah!*"

Her attention had been caught by another spearman. A new technique! She craned forward in her seat. Utterly new! The man, a left-hander, grasped the spear one third from the butt with immovable right hand and with his left worked the butt up and down, sideways, in circles. At twice the speed of the butt the spear-head flashed in rapid feints, reversing each movement of the butt. The adversary, unaccustomed to this unorthodox, pivoting action, gave ground with the spear stabbing at his ears, his toes, till he was in full flight. The crowd roared their amusement.

After some further skirmishing the men with the spears were adjudged the winners, though not without some protest from those of the audience who had pledged their money on the shield-men. The arena was cleared by way of the west gate.

A moment's pause, then a trumpet blowing to the four corners of the theater gave notice that the next spectacle would be seven male slaves from Greece, tribute from conquered lands, against a black bull from west of Zafare.

Inas saw Ariadne straighten on her cushioned seat, saw that the knuckles of her hands were white where she gripped them together. Then the princess turned and scanned the group behind her. In a moment she caught Inas' eye and motioned that the girl come and sit beside her.

"Pretend that I have called you to adjust a lock of my hair," she murmured. Inas knew that the princess was deeply stirred by the coming event.

The western gates opened again and amid the silence of the audience the Greeks were herded in. They stood, feet stockily planted, chests up, facing the not unfriendly crowd; but a striking contrast to the Cretans who had just left. They looked soiled and tattered in the same loose, unfitted garments they had worn in the Hall of the Labrys, their feet shod in cowhide sandals strapped halfway to the knee. In their hands, ready for action, they held the usual short, bronze Cretan sword.

A moment of suspense, then the eastern gate swung wide and a large black bull trotted in. He paused, with his suspicious little red eyes that blinked in the light, sullenly eyeing the arena.

Inas judged the bull as not one of the best. Too heavy and short in the low haunches, too brief as to horn to make good sport. But his coat had been brushed and oiled to glistening perfection, he wore a garland of geraniums glowing against his shoulders, and his gilded horns glittered royally.

Theseus, with his friends behind him, faced the animal with an immovable stubbornness that was almost comic, more bull-like than the bull himself. He seemed almost to be fighting the beast by sheer will power, human will pitted against that of the great black animal before him.

The pause lengthened. "Isn't he magnificent!" murmured Ariadne.

"Isn't he *stupid!*" thought Inas. "Why doesn't he play the beast?"

The audience evidently echoed her thought, for faint *boos* and *ahs* of derision, began to rise, to grow louder as the people became impatient for some action.

"Didn't anyone tell him what to do?" thought the girl. "*Ah . . . !*"

The animal had turned away to trot once around the arena; then with increasing speed again. At last, perhaps because of some betraying movement, his attention was caught by the waiting Greeks. He wheeled and trotted straight toward them with lowered head. But a defiant gesture on the part of Theseus caused the beast to pause and eye this strange, hulking man before him. Flinging up his head the animal turned and started to pass for the third time, but near enough now for the Greek, by a step, to reach him. The strong arm was extended, and with a blow that could be heard to the farthest seat in the circus Theseus brought down his sword on the neck of the beast. The animal fell as though struck by lightning.

"Wonderful!" murmured Ariadne, on the edge of her seat.

"Idiot!" muttered Inas between her teeth. "*Butcher!* Does he think this is a barn, or a meat stall!"

Again the crowd seemed to be of her mind. Boos and whistles roared and shrilled from the topmost seats. But with a gesture of scorn Theseus herded his little band into a corner and stood silently defying the crowd. Again the mules were driven in, nets attached to the slaughtered body and the bull dragged away. This would later be cut and roasted and given to the poor of the city.

Sprinklers came, fresh earth was spread over the place where blood had flowed, and the trumpets announced a second contest between bull and Greeks. This bull also was big and heavy, black with white feet and a white nose; and, like the last one, not the best type for bull-vaulting. He entered the ring warily, as one who had been there before, then seeing the Greeks, made a swift dash for them, scattering them wildly. In a moment four of them were in a mad race for the further corners of the arena. Bewildered, the beast paused, not knowing which to follow, then wheeling tried first one, then another, but at each turn was deflected from his purpose by the flutter of a garment in another direction.

One lad, the youngest of the Greeks, was in full stretch down the length of the arena with the bull after him when Theseus tore off his tunic and threw it flapping into the face of the running beast, then before he could shake it off had slain him with that mighty arm.

"Fisherman! Is it thus that he catches fish!" jeered the crowd. Inas wriggled uncomfortably. Indeed that was not considered good tactics in the ring, to blind the eye of the opposing bull.

By now the audience was thoroughly bored. They wanted skill, the light lithe acrobatics of the trained Cretan bull-vaulter, not the crude actions of this clumsy barbarian of a countryman.

"Take him out!" called someone. "Away with the Greeks!" called another, and the cry, taken up, passed swiftly around the circle. Theseus, unaware of the crowd's jeering hostility, still stood heavily on his heels, legs wide spread, defying his captors. Only the princess seemed to thrill to his bigness, to his clumsy masculinity. Inas watched her and wondered.

Three bulls had been commanded for the Greeks. As the trumpeter announced the third entry the crowd fell silent. Perhaps this would be better. Certainly the animal was of a different breed.

He trotted briskly into the ring, eyeing his audience with the amiable air of a friendly puppy, shook his beribboned locks and twinkled cheerily from bright brown eyes. His horns had the perfect backward action for an acrobat's bull, his body was not too heavy, his legs slim and quick.

"Oh!" cried Inas involuntarily. "What a pity! I do hope he doesn't kill that little white bull!"

Ariadne faced her furiously. "Be still, girl!" she commanded. Inas dropped her eyes and reddened. She hadn't meant to speak aloud.

Theseus was weary by this time. He faced the new animal defiantly, waiting for its first move. But the little white bull was apparently eager for a game. Each time the Greek got close enough to extend his arm in the death blow, the animal would wheel and, with a sniff almost of derision, trot away.

"Play him, play him!" shouted the audience.

But Theseus had no understanding of the tongue, no comprehension of the game he was supposed to play. And moment by moment the crowd's sympathy swung to the little bull. This was indeed too good an animal for such as Theseus.

Then the eastern door swung open and the guards entered. Someone had given an order, perhaps the prince, perhaps even Minos who was himself a connoisseur of the game. The Greeks were herded to one side and the bull urged gently, with long strong rods, through the doorway. Theseus and his youths were again alone in the arena.

Then someone threw a cushion, a brilliant crimson cushion, into the ring.

"This for thy ease and comfort," shrilled a Cretan voice. The crowd roared with laughter. But Theseus raised the pillow, made a sardonic bow toward the audience and as the western gate opened for the Greeks, made his exit, the pillow under his arm; not, Inas thought, completely without glory. He had at least shown courage.

CHAPTER NINE

THE BLACK BULL TOSSES

The thirty novices were grouped into six teams, five in a team. And as in all the circus games there was much betting among the audience as to the winning teams. Each group was led by a boy, but whether his group contained more boys or more girls mattered not at all, since the bull-vaulting depended not so much on actual strength as on timing, and speed, and agility. At these a girl was likely to be as skillful as a boy.

Both groups, and their time of entering the ring, were decided by the casting of lots. Naturally each novice wished to be with the group he knew best, and Inas was glad to find Hana among her five for the first entry. A tall boy named Nex, son of a master blacksmith and as skillful as he was strong, Mimas, slim and lithe, but erratic, and Arkamanthus, oldest of the novices, made up the little team. She had worked with all save Arkamanthus and knew their weak points. Her success depended as much on them as on her own skill and she must watch Arkamanthus in the first game, try to learn his methods of playing the bull.

Her team drew second place in the ring on this, their first day. That was better than being last. The novices waited in a small room off the entrance gate, where slaves again rubbed them with oil till their brown bodies glistened, where ribbons and knots were retied and sandal straps readjusted, lest they work loose and cause a fall in the ring. Their hands were also rubbed with resin that they might better grip the long slippery horns of the charging bull.

The quiet room was like the pulsing heart of a storm. Shouts, calls, the applause of the crowd outside came dimly on the hot air and with an odd impersonal quality. One could hear the thud and rush of hoof beats in the ring and the softened roar of other bulls waiting their turn across the arena. What bull would they draw first? Inas wondered and wished for the little white one that had been saved from the Greeks. There was a good bull, with a quick, lively toss of the head that would throw one backward into a perfect somersault.

So when they finally entered the ring and found that they had been allotted the little white bull it seemed indeed that the gods had answered her prayer. He came trotting out, playful, yet fierce; fierce enough to charge with the necessary speed, not at all stubborn or in need of teasing. That saved much time. When a bull must be nagged into moving, when he turns his back on the circus and will not budge from his corner, then half the time is spent in coaxing him into the proper mood for a charge and the performers are worn and nervous before the game has commenced.

For a moment Inas felt a return of her old stage-fright. Never before had she played in the ring, like this, but always in the open field, or on the training ground. Then glancing at Hana she saw that the girl's hands were shaking, that her lips were pale with fright. Hana's courage before the bull was unquestioned. She too must be afraid of the audience.

"Courage!" whispered Inas. "We are not Greek slaves, to face the bull without knowledge or skill." Hana gave a feeble smile but the color began to flow back into her bluish lips.

"I'll take him first," volunteered Inas. "Do you, Arkamanthus, make the first leap. I'll prepare the way for you."

The little animal was started around the ring by a sharp clap on the rump. He came charging toward them, but he must be made to lower his horns, else the handgrip would be wrong. Inas danced lightly ahead, this way, that way, teasing him on, spatting her hands together, turning now and then to look back. She whistled a few provocative notes, shrill and clear. Twice the bull tossed gilded horns at her, but each time she stepped nimbly aside. He was not yet in the proper mood for a good toss.

Then Arkamanthus took him over. A few moments more, then . . . ah . . . Hana had made the first leap. Not very good, but fair; enough to rid the child of her momentary fears. Mimas caught her as she left the back of the bull and the animal, feeling something alien brush his shoulders, charged forward, shaking glittering horns in the hot sunlight.

He was hers this time. Inas had a moment when she was aware of the sun on her back, warm and pleasant, of the crowd above her, restlessly shifting, of the scent of damp earth and the resin that hardened on her hands. But all sound, all color, seemed concentrated in this ring. Then the bull's head was down—would it be far enough or should she step aside, wait for him to come again? Yes, she had it. Gilt on the horns was not so good a grip as the bare horn itself. Now the quick toss over, up . . . up, her head touching the bull's as he raised her with his own swift action of the neck, then, head downward, as when one dives. Here was Inas' own special strength, since her diving had made her careless of whether she stood on her head or her feet. A quick run along the back of the bull, then she landed lightly on the ground. A perfect somersault.

The crowd roared with delight, but Inas heard nothing.

Arkamanthus was the next. But the bull tossed sideways, and though the boy made a clean landing, it was only after a left-handed twist over the animal's back.

For a while then the little bull would not put his head down, but trotted this way and that, eyeing them suspiciously, quizzically. Did he know perhaps that in the end he would be only a sacrifice to Rhea? Inas felt a little sorry for the white bull.

Then he caught the flutter of Inas' kilt and came toward her, head angrily lowered. She seized the horns . . . over . . . over . . . and a clean landing into the outstretched arms of Arkamanthus, who stiffened and held her above his head, waving and smiling, before he dropped her lightly to the sand. That was good. The crowd always loved variations, little dance steps, clowning, in the ring. But it must all be done within the strict formality of the rules. None of your Greek clumsiness here. And the audience knew. Many and many of them had been among the bull-vaulters in their younger days.

Some of them, long ago and not so long ago, had been famous in the ring. There was, for instance, Tanthomes, who had done the double somersault on the bull's back and won the golden fillet for it, all on such a day as this. Inas herself had tried it, many and many a time, and knew its almost-impossibility. The bull must be just so, horns wide and low, everything else being perfect, and the toss a long and deep one to augment the extraordinary skill of the performer.

The little white bull was tiring now. Soon they would be free and another group would enter the ring. Once more he faced in Inas' direction. Once more she made a good leap. Applause. Then the doorway to the dressing-rooms, a rubdown with warm oil, mats in the corner and a blessed sleep.

That night in the palace room where the girls slept, Inas heard comparisons of one group with another. No team was allowed to see the work of the others, lest an accident prove too demoralizing, but from what she could learn her own team had done as well as any. One boy had been badly gored by a bull and had been withdrawn from the game. One girl had a sprained ankle and two others had been slightly injured, enough to necessitate their absence from the Bull Ring. These changes of course would break up the teams.

New lots were drawn, the groups shifted, and on the following night another regrouping was made. On the morning of the third day Inas found herself with three boys and with Hana facing the first bull of the morning's show.

He was a gigantic black creature with a swirl of white behind the gilt rosette that decorated his forehead, one white leg, and a supremely wicked temper. He came trotting, head up, fierce little eyes gleaming redly, into the center of the ring without the usual pause to survey it. Tossing his horns he swung madly down the arena, and Inas stepped sideways to allow one of the boys to take him. Kanthros was good, but the greater and unconscious strength of his right arm threw him a fraction off balance, so that only by an awkward twist did he land upright.

A groan arose from those among the crowd who had wagers on this team. And someone, against all orders, threw a rose-wreath into the ring. The bull pawed the damp ground, then plunged forward, tossing the wreath, to trample it with furious hoofs.

Inas again. This time she was directly in line for the long, wicked horns and saw them lower toward her. For a long moment time stood still. With seeming deliberation she grasped the horns, felt them rise with apparent slowness and her body straighten, upside down, on the long glittering spikes. Then the pace forward, weight thrown back. But such a toss! Never had she known such a toss! She seemed, looking down, to be more than a body's height from the long back with its gleaming swirls of black hair, and in that seeming retardation of time she could distinguish the ripple of each muscle beneath the shining skin.

Gathering all her force, and with that same strange and apparent deliberation, she doubled herself into a ball, knees drawn up to chin, and hurled herself again—there was almost, but not quite, time enough for a third spin. Her will checked and rejected the idea before her muscles could begin to put it into execution. Right side up again she poised, hands on the bull's back for the whisper of a second, then, using his forward action to propel her, she leaped forward, to land on the rigidly outheld arms of Kanthros. Slowly her toes touched the earth.

Only then, with the crash of voices, of cheers and wild shouts, did she realize again the audience above her; realize that she had done the almost-impossible trick of the ancient Tanthomes. She had turned a double somersault on the back of a charging bull.

CHAPTER TEN

THE FAIR

That night for the first time the graduates, no longer novices, were free to go to the fair. All week its music and its drums, its strange scents and sounds, the babble of voices and the shouts of the hucksters had called to them from the low sloping banks of the river. Now, as though they were children let out of school, they could wrap their cloaks about them and scatter through the stalls and the trading booths.

It was growing dusk and sunset was flaming behind the mountains when Inas came out on the palace steps and passed the giant, armed soldier on guard there. Someone waited by the path to the river, someone in a long cloak and high strapped boots. The boy turned as she descended the steps, and she saw that it was Kadmos.

"Will you and your fine gold wreath visit the fair with a humble sailor?" he asked.

Inas laughed and by way of answer slipped her hand into his arm and gave a little skip of pleasure. "I looked for you the first day of the circus and then was too busy to look again. Were you there?"

Kadmos grunted assent but she knew that he was pleased at her winning of the fillet. Now she slipped it from her hair and paused on the pathway to display its beauty of workmanship, the finest in all Crete.

"And Kres was the maker." She dimpled with amusement. "How angry he must be that it has gone to the daughter of Daidalos." She caressed the wreath with the tip of one finger, her mouth curling in half conscious pride of ownership. It was a delicate intertwining of sea-shells with the tendrils of seaweed and formed with such marvelous art it seemed as though the very works of nature had been skillfully overlaid with the craftsman's gold.

"I know it well." Kadmos gestured curtly that she return it to her hair. "Has it not hung, for all the years of our lives, among the finest works of the gold beaters? But why should there be hatred between Daidalos and Kres, two of the greatest men in Crete?"

Inas shrugged. "I know not the beginning of the hatred, but many things have gone to ripen it. Daidalos was always lacking in tact and diplomacy, Kres always jealous of my father's success. The gold worker was chief to oppose him when he built the north gate of the palace. In fact Kres, then high in favor because of the Bull Cups he had just completed and a gaming board he had made for Minos, so influenced the king that the work was ordered to cease."

"A gold worker's opinion on the strength of a nation's walls!" Kadmos spoke with bitterness, as always, on this point.

Inas again slipped her hand into his. "Come, let us visit the fair before darkness comes. They say it is a fair such as Knossos has never seen; men from Egypt and from the north, from the islands to the south and west and fruits and treasures and games such as Crete has never known. Have you seen it?"

"Only a little," he admitted, restored to good humor by Inas' change of subject. "I waited to see it all with you."

The sound of the crowded fairgrounds rose clear on the chill evening air. A little breeze stirred the fringe of curls beneath the gold wreath and Inas lifted her hand to ask a blessing of the new moon, just seen above the tip of the eastern hills, then patted the bag of shell coinage at her waist. Each contestant in the games had been well rewarded, whether among the losers or winners.

Tonight she planned to purchase a gift for Teeta, a thin collar for the kitten, and something for Daidalos, though his desires were so few and so hard to satisfy. Perhaps, even, she might find something for Kadmos. She glanced at him through slanting lashes. How well he looked tonight with his long swinging cloak, the bright scarf about his slim waist, the long locks that hung in formal black curls to his broad shoulders. Here was no plowman or shepherd from the barbarous hills of Greece. Kadmos was all Cretan and proud of his splendid heritage.

The sky was still bright, pale green fading into a gold that outlined the western hills. But the gold was drowned at the outskirts of the fairgrounds by the thousands of torches and lamps that lit the hundreds of booths and stalls. Traders cried their wares, competing with each other for the attention of passers-by, and contests and games of all sorts were in full swing. Those who had wagered on the circus and had won would risk their gains for still further profits and those who had lost, but not all, strove to win back some of it.

At almost the first stall they paused to examine, Inas' bright locks and the gold fillet made her an object of attention and pressing curiosity, almost of veneration. For many of these people she had been the cause of winning great sums on the games, and others, who might have lost, still felt that she had done a miraculous thing, an achievement never duplicated by any woman in the ring, and by few men. Inas, in her own mind, gave most credit to the bull and to that strange combination of perfect timing, or luck and chance and a dozen other elements. But it was soon apparent that the people of Knossos thought otherwise.

As swiftly as she was recognized, a small crowd began to gather behind Kadmos and the girl. Little boys and girls pressed close to touch her, jostling good-naturedly for the honor of fingering her cloak, begging for just one lock of her strange golden hair which was possibly of the precious metal itself. Many of these people, easterners from the further cities of the island, had never before beheld a blond.

Voices called to voices across the alleys of the stalls. Small boys, half-grown youths, shoved and danced before her. Inas soon found it impossible to stop and gaze where she wished to purchase, so tightly packed became the crowd behind her, and she soon gave up the idea of buying gifts for Daidalos and the others. One experience was sufficient.

This happened at a goldsmith's booth. Rings and bracelets of tinsel gilt and of bronze were intermingled with more precious things; strange bits of amber with flies embedded in their lovely translucent depths, little trinkets of carved coral, delicate as lace, arms and hands, hearts and fishes; amulets to offer as thanks at the altar of Rhea, and long chains of worked gold, delicate flower patterns, shells and strange sea creatures intertwined.

Inas paused here in admiration and slipped her hand from Kadmos' arm. "The price of that chain?" she asked, pointing to one of expert craftsmanship, daisies with petals overlapping to form a necklace.

"That one—" The merchant crouching before his wares lifted the chain with two long bony fingers and dangled it before her admiring eyes. "Take it, O Princess of Bull-Vaulters." And as Inas drew back in protest, "Take it and bring blessings upon my household. Today in the circus I won the price of a dozen such chains as this."

Kadmos interrupted brusquely, "I will buy her the chain. Give it to me."

But the merchant's desire was so eager, so genuine, that the girl felt it would be an insult to refuse. Reluctantly she took the gift and wound it about her neck, resolving to ask no more the price of things she wished to buy. If, she told Kadmos, she saw anything she wished she would send Teeta later to purchase it. "Though it is a bit unpleasant to be so conspicuous, just because I have yellow hair and wear the bull-vaulter's wreath."

"Come, let us escape this rabble." Kadmos pulled at her wrist, indicating an alley between two deserted stalls. "Once we have lost this crowd, cover your hair with your scarf, that we may avoid further attention."

Luck was with them. Slipping between the darkened booths and keeping to the dimmer unlighted ways, they wandered undetected for a while.

Here, in the moving crowd and among the traders, were freed Greeks, and others, who were serfs, held booths and traded for

their masters' profit. Here were tall Sudanese from the lands beyond the Nile, and Phenicians who sailed over the edge of the
world in small, square-winged boats with cargoes of precious
amber, and returned laden with black tin, perfumes, and musk.
Here were goldsmiths' apprentices tending stalls while their masters sat over the evening meal. The booths glowed with the yellow
metal in cups and chalices, and lamps and wreaths and crowns
and chains and anklets. Here were piles of fine linen so sheer
one could pass it between the loop of finger and thumb, and colored with the dye of the murex shells for which Crete was known
throughout the world. Some of this linen was deep purple, some
was rosy with the hue of early dawn, some was woven sheer with
threads of gold, and some had silver in it. Strange dark men,
heavy of thigh and hip, sold arrows and slings from the west
coast, and there were contests of skill with the bow and spear,
that purchasers might try their weapon before paying good shell
coins in exchange.

On a flat place, hard trodden by many feet, down near the
silently flowing water many men and women danced the slow,
meandering dance of Crete. Inas would have liked to join them
and plucked at Kadmos' cloak, but he shook his head. Well, perhaps it was wiser not.

So they passed on among the further booths down by the
river, with their sun covers of roughly woven rush mattings—
unlighted, dark hulks against the stars. Here the meat markets
and grain markets began, and here were stalled the cattle, sheep,
and goats, all folded for the night and silent save for the usual
beast noises.

"There is nothing here," Inas told the boy. "Let us return
among the people."

On the fringe of the grounds was a booth where bows and arrows were sold. No one was buying now, and Inas' curls were hidden beneath her scarf. Would it be safe, she wondered, to try her skill at the target?

Kadmos was willing, so she bought three arrows. This was a game that she loved. She had shot at ducks along the shore, had gone hunting for gazelle and wild goats on the hills with Glos, and once, with Daidalos, she had even made her own bows and arrows. Now she chose her bow carefully from the half-dozen in the booth, tested the springiness of the draw and the weight of the weapon and asked that the two torches be moved to throw a better light on the upright bundle of rushes that was fixed in the earth to serve as a target.

She slipped the notched, unfeathered arrow into the bow and raised it to her shoulder. The target was marked off in distances from top to bottom, each the width of a hand, and was narrow, half the width of a hand across. She aimed at the center marking, but her arrow flew wide, barely lodging in the outer edge of the rushes. With the second arrow she struck the center of the target, the third edged it so closely that they quivered together.

"Now yours." She passed the bow to Kadmos.

He shook his head. "Sailors have little skill with such weapons." But on her insistence Kadmos chose another bow, heavier and longer, and picked his arrows with care. Then aiming slowly, he drew the cord, let loose the arrow. It went wide, wider than her first.

"Better success on the second. It takes one or two to get the range," she reminded him. Again he aimed and drew, but the second arrow was flawed and did not follow his aim.

"The last may be the lucky one," Inas consoled him. "That

arrow was crooked from birth." She wished ruefully that she had not suggested the game, or had purposely shot with less skill. The third arrow, aimed and drawn, struck on the edge of the inner section. None had gone close to the center as her second and last. Kadmos placed the bow on the ground and paid for the game. They turned away toward the center of the fair again.

For a while now they had gone unrecognized. Inas drew the scarf tighter about her hair, and they pressed again through the crowds that thronged the alleys. It was growing late and many merchants were extinguishing their torches, curling up in blankets to sleep or guard their wares till dawn. They came to a small stand where strange fruit was on sale, little golden balls of a tangy, juicy sweetness, from the far slopes of the Black Sea. Inas touched them with a finger. Teeta would love such a gift.

"How much?" she asked the trader.

Cross-legged among his bright spilled fruit he glanced up indifferently, quoted a price. Inas was too much a child of the Mediterranean to take the asked amount as selling price. She countered with an offer of half that sum. In the harsh accent of eastern Crete the merchant lowered his demand.

Kadmos plucked at her sleeve. "Come away," he urged in a low voice. Inas twitched away from his fingers.

"In a moment," she promised and leaned over to count as many oranges as she could carry in the slack of her scarf. Two long pale curls escaped from their covering and swung down before the eyes of the astonished trader. He gave a sudden grin of recognition.

"The fruit is yours and at your own price," he assured her. Then peering beyond he must have glimpsed some friend or relative from his own corner of the island. Raising his arm he let out a shout of greeting. Here was good business for his stall.

"Come! Come! Here is the Golden Maid, the Fortunate One! Come and touch her that you may have success and fortune for the year!"

Inas, startled, dropped the oranges, and turning to flee, was suddenly surrounded by a wall of people. It was as though the very ground had thrown forth humans. Strange creatures, uncouth, skin-clad, muttering in a dialect she scarcely understood, pressed round her, jostled and shoved to touch her hair. Someone caught a lock of it and pulled relentlessly as though that bright amulet might come free in his hand. With tears of pain starting in her eyes, she wrapped her arms about her head for protection and screamed.

Where was Kadmos? For a moment the crowd had separated them. Now, with head down, arms flailing, elbows and knees and even teeth in action, he came charging toward her, fighting his way through the noisy, wrestling throng. Unprepared, the crowd wavered. Kadmos had an instant to grasp hold of the girl's wrist and drag her free. They took to their heels, racing, weaving right and left through the darkened alleys.

Behind them a cry, mistaken but dangerous, "Thief! Robber!" had started suddenly. Then a steady thud of footsteps and the pack was in full cry.

Inas was in excellent training, as was Kadmos. They could easily have outdistanced their pursuers if those pursuers had all been behind them. But the cry had spread on ahead and, as Inas and Kadmos swept by stall after stall, people began to turn and stare. It was only a matter of seconds before they would be stopped by some countryman, quicker than his fellows.

"Oh, Kadmos, what shall we do?"

"Just a moment—I have an idea—just a moment." The boy spoke easily, soothingly, and pulled her aside into a darkened street with all booths closed for the night. For the moment they had outdistanced the mob, but directly ahead lay one of the main streets of the fair, bright with torches, still thronging with people.

"*Thief! . . . Robber!*" the hoarse shout swept ahead.

They emerged from the side street and forced their way into the crowd. Almost directly before them, full in the light of a flaring torch, stood a man alone. Tall, spare, with beaked nose, thin mouth, sunken cheeks. Quickly he glanced behind him.

"Now let us see what his conscience is worth," muttered Kadmos. Arm out he pointed, raising the shout, "Stop thief! Stop him!" Like a flame among dry leaves the cry was taken up, spread back to the onrushing throng. Kadmos pulled the girl aside, stuffed her without ceremony into the corner of a deserted stall and, dropping to the ground, hauled her down beside him. His strong arm gave her comfort and protection.

The man who was accused, after one startled glance at the onrush of pursuers, had turned and fled, taking great strides on skinny, ancient legs. The crowd, glad to have their victim so plainly labeled for them, rushed past. There was a cloud of dust, a swirl of footsteps. Kadmos and Inas were left alone.

Inas sat up. In the dim light she seemed breathless, heaving with great sobs that shook her slim body. She hiccuped, choked, and drew away from Kadmos' friendly thumping hand.

Concerned, he put his arm around her. "It's all right. Do not worry. Inas, stop, I say! You'll be ill!"

"No . . . no. I'm all right." Inas gulped, controlled her emotion, though tears streamed unchecked down her face. "Oh, Kadmos . . . did . . . did you see . . . see his f-face!" It was giggles, not fear that shook her. Kadmos, puzzled, pulled away.

"No, who was it? The thief you mean?"

"Y-yes." For another moment Inas struggled for words, then spoke demurely. "Yes, though it was no thief. That was Kres, head of the gold workers. What a very bad conscience that man must have!"

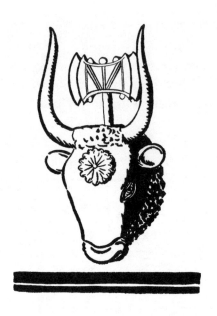

CHAPTER ELEVEN

THE SLAVE AUCTION

Her father's workshop had always been for Inas a place both of amusement and of wonder. It occupied a crowded, cluttered corner of the open and airy portico and was always overflowing the bounds set for it and being sternly checked by the irreverent Teeta. On shelves and work-benches was a mélange of inventions, some discarded, some never completed, all testifying to the fertility and breadth of Daidalos' imagination and interest.

There was a strange collection of wheels, such as those from a chariot, but of varying sizes, and connected by an odd arrangement of calfskin belts. One could turn, slowly and with difficulty, a handle at the nearest end and at the further end, for no apparent reason, a small wheel spun madly with incredible speed. This arrangement was interesting to work, but Inas had never discovered its purpose. From nails in the wall hung various objects: a net for fishermen, with its meshes of unequal size; some experiments of bronze welded into a sort of sandal for horse or mule; other things of bronze such as a new pivot for the heavy Cretan doors—this arranged to swing the door open more easily.

Today the inventor was experimenting with a piece of cord hung from a low beam above his head. Beside him sat a basket full of spindle whorls, those small objects with which the spinner weights the thread on her distaff while she twirls it with busy thumb and forefinger. From the cord Daidalos had hung a light strip of bamboo, sideways, through a notch cut in its center.

Carefully he went through the pottery whorls till he had picked out two that seemed the lightest and tied one with a thin thread to one end of the bamboo . . . the other to the opposite end. Then he chipped a little pottery dust from one whorl until it balanced the other and the bamboo hung as before, swinging exactly even. Next he removed them and exchanged the two whorls. Again they swung, balancing.

Inas, chin in hands and elbows on knees as she perched on the railing, watched the whole process with absorbed interest.

"That is fortunate indeed, as they might not have been equal when exchanged," remarked Daidalos.

"Why fortunate?" she asked. "Does it matter whether one spindle whorl is equal to another so long as each swings evenly when spun?"

"This," he explained, touching the bamboo so that it vibrated gently under his finger, "is a device to estimate the weight of things, that objects may be balanced against each other whether the space they occupy is much or little. Sticky things, like honey, and things with strange shapes, like fowls, are difficult to pour into a measure, whereby traders cheat honest citizens."

Inas settled herself more comfortably on her perch. She loved her father's explanations. "In the king's storehouse there are small weights that measure the gold. Would not weights of different sizes be confusing to people, common people who buy in the markets? And who, to weigh a goat, would wish to carry another goat about with him?"

Daidalos smiled and explained further. "But a thing may be weighed without remembering many weights, and by a lesser weight than itself. See!"

As he talked he had been checking spindle whorls till he had twenty that seemed of similar weight. Next he tied each with a thread in a little loop and attached those twenty to one end of the bamboo, so that they hung from the same notch at the top. At the further end the single whorl flew up sharply.

Inas, pressing close to see, chuckled. "But by your own act you disprove what you say! The twenty far outweighs the one."

"Wait." Daidalos slid the bar along the loop of cord from the ceiling, slid it till but a small measure of the bar was at the end with the twenty whorls, slid it till the two ends balanced again. Then, a twinkle in his eye, he looked at Inas for her approval. "What now?" he said.

He removed one of the twenty whorls, made a nick in the rod where the one, counterbalancing the twenty, hung on the bamboo, then slid it along till it counterbalanced the nineteen. Then he removed another whorl and slid the further one till it counterbalanced the eighteen. So he continued, making small nicks for each move.

When he had made the last cut he turned, smiling, to Inas. "Behold, if you will, a gift for Ariadne. Thus may she measure, by weight, the yarn, whether spun or unspun, that no dealer, by fluffing the wool, or by loose winding of the thread, may cheat her."

"Or give it rather to Minos, the king. We women have little time for toys!" came a caustic voice from the doorway. "Measures such as our mothers used were given us by the gods themselves and should last unchanged for our children's children."

Daidalos, for a moment slightly crestfallen, caught his daughter's eye and grinned cheerfully. "No trader in all Knossos could cheat thy eagle eye, O Teeta!"

But Inas, suppressing her laughter, had noted that Teeta brought a message from the palace, one of those small, oblong slabs of baked clay which would bear on its surface of thin wax the writing of the king himself. Teeta placed the slab in Daidalos' hand and together father and daughter bent over it. Teeta departing, remarked, "There is also a fine jar of wine." Minos always sent a gift with his message. The message was simple, merely a summons for Daidalos to appear at the palace in the morning.

"I also will go then," decided Inas, "and return to Ariadne the ring of the priestess and the deer."

That ring had lain heavily on her conscience. She had forgotten it once, when she had returned to Ariadne with word of Theseus. When she had gone back to the palace before the bull-vaulting she had known that then she would have no opportunity to be alone with the princess and it was far too valuable to send by any messenger. Such a seal from the hand of the king or of one of his family endowed the wearer, for the time, with almost royal power. He was the representative of the king himself, or, as in this case, of the princess, and the ring must be obeyed. One did not lightly despatch such power by a messenger, no matter how trustworthy.

For safe-keeping, meanwhile, she had hidden it in an odd little
box of carved olive wood, one that had come long ago with her
mother from Greece. Now she went to seek it.

Yes, it was secure and snug in its wrapping of violet yarn. Inas
touched it with a pointed finger, then slipped it on the first finger of her left hand. The circle was heavy, decorated with a bead-
ing of minute gold drops, beautifully regular. The seal itself was a
long oval, smooth at the edge, exquisitely molded with a minute
deer, very slim on prancing legs, very delicate as to neck and nos-
tril. Beside him was a tiny priestess, offering sacrifice at an altar
but turning her gaze on the deer at her side.

This too was possibly the work of Kres or of some one of his
immediate workmen. No man in all Crete did work of such delicate finish and beauty. Inas removed it and slipped it into the box
with a little sigh of regret. Of course she could not wear it.

Early next morning when Daidalos called her, "Hasten, if you
would come to the palace with me," she went to the box again.
The ring was gone!

Stolen! Surely no one of Daidalos' household could be a thief.
Any servant of the place might indeed enter and leave her room
without comment; the door was never locked. Teeta, who had
been a second mother to her? Mufu, who, though mischievous,
was of proved integrity? The extra half-dozen maids and men
who worked about the place, tended the mules, carried Teeta's
market basket, prepared the vegetables for the kitchen—any of
them might have taken it . . . but would they?

"Hasten, daughter!" called Daidalos from the court. "It draws
close to the hour for my meeting with the king."

Inas' hands were shaking as she mechanically tightened the
scarf over the gold fillet that bound her hair, and sped down the
stairs. Should she tell her father of the loss, ask his advice and

assistance in finding the ring? No, she thought, as they passed up the sloping street toward the upper town, better first to take what measures she could. Perhaps Teeta had thought it merely a foolish gift from Kadmos and had placed it elsewhere for greater safety, perhaps the kitten had knocked the cover from the box and the ring had rolled to some crevice in the stone flooring . . . perhaps . . . Inas frowned in concentration. Suppose Ariadne remembered to ask for it today!

But Daidalos had news that might be, to Ariadne, of greater concern than the loss of the ring. He seldom listened to gossip of the court, but this had interest for him because it concerned his own work, the Labyrinth.

"Last night," he told Inas, "the Greek slaves tried to escape."

"The Greek slaves!" gasped Inas. "But—"

"Teeta has been telling me the gossip of the market," Daidalos related with some amusement at himself. "One of the Greeks, the leader—"

"That would be Theseus," Inas was certain.

"Theseus was the name. This Theseus led a group of men who beset the guard bringing them their evening meal. Then they overcame the second guard at the door—"

"With bare hands? They were unarmed."

"Such is the tale. They fought their way down the corridor toward the stairway but became confused in the twistings and windings of the passages and were captured again."

"But they are simple, those passages," Inas protested. "One leads merely into the next one."

"Simple? Yes, for folk who have lived always in many-roomed dwellings. But the Greeks' houses are of but one room or, at the most, two-roomed huts of logs. To them the passages must seem a maze, built for bewilderment."

"That is true," Inas remarked thoughtfully. She could well imagine Theseus leaping on the guard, killing a man with his bare hands, then racing through the winding hallways to become as bewildered and lost as a bull in the passages of a bull pen.

Daidalos strode so rapidly that Inas had some difficulty to equal his pace. Turning into the road that led from Knossos to the hilltop, they became part of the stream of people thronging toward the palace: traders, petitioners, men with goods to deliver, laborers, slaves and freemen of all colors and many nations.

"And then?" asked Inas, returning to the matter of the Greeks. "Was Theseus slain?"

"Some reports say that he was. Others in the market say 'no.' But the slaves are soon to be sold, that they may be scattered and their strength broken up. I envy not the man that buys this Theseus, if he still lives. A pity," he commented, thinking aloud. "They might all have escaped, at least as far as the Greek boats below the town. For in the other angle of that passageway, opposite to the one they must have taken, a door swings open to an old pathway down the steep bank toward the river."

"Oh, Father, how do you know?"

"It was there when I rebuilt the passages, some five seasons ago. Undoubtedly it is still there. None knew of it then. Two workmen and myself came upon a hinged stone that swung outward when pressed upon. No doubt an exit planned years ago by that Daidalos who was my grandfather; a way out in case of siege or disaster to the palace. But what king, nowadays, would dream of danger for his people or his court?"

Inas knew this grievance of her father's and tactfully suggested, "Kadmos also thinks as you do, that Minos is overconfident of his power, sending his fleet for trade and gold when it should be kept for the defense of his people." She dropped her voice as she spoke, since who could tell what man among all this throng might overhear and use even such casual comment as a weapon against the speaker?

"Indeed?" Daidalos expressed his surprise. "Kadmos said that? I had not thought a man of action would have leisure for thought. Indeed!" He seemed to ponder on that till they reached the steps of the palace itself.

The sentry at the outer gate was struggling with two men who drove a dozen heavily laden donkeys. The tradesmen, sellers of the mats with which their beasts were loaded, spoke no word of the Cretan tongue, and the sentry, whose face was perspiring from his efforts, strove to explain to them that the mats must be unrolled and examined by him before they could pass into the palace courtyard.

Amused at his troubles, Inas paused to watch a moment. Once a foreign "ambassador" had concealed a dwarf, armed with a deadly poisoned spear within a similar bale of rugs. The trick had been discovered before the rug reached Minos, for whom it was intended as a gift, but since then more rigid precautions had been in effect.

The sentry, with a brief glance at Daidalos, gave Inas a wry smile, then turned back to his duties.

Within the gate the passage branched, one way leading to the workshops and quarters of the artisans, the other to the main palace buildings. Here, past two tall black soldiers from the lands to the south, was the entrance to cool wide hallways where plashing water echoed pleasantly. The halls, with their narrow-based pillars, were decorated with battle shields of black and white spotted cowhide, and the painted roof-beams were inlaid intricately with pearl and rose quartz. Curtained doorways led to rooms beyond rooms, and low, shallow-stepped blind stairways, scattered with rugs and cushions, served as pleasant seats against the painted walls.

At a wide court surrounding a central fountain Daidalos paused and, meeting an attendant, parted from Inas. Minos was ever an early riser and Inas knew her father would not have long to wait.

The private stairway leading to the princess's apartments was further along. Inas was halfway up the shallow steps when she paused at the sound of a voice below her.

"Then to Zathess shall the girl go!"

Slowly she mounted to the corridor at the top with its decorations of flying-fishes and sea birds and overlooking, on its further side, a large open court. Pausing here behind a pillar, Inas looked down.

The court, shaded from the early sun by its high eastern wall, was half full. Some fifty men sat or stood against two sides of the yard and on the third side, raised on a small platform of three steps, was a dark, foreign-looking man clad in a full-skirted coat of red-dyed goatskin and holding a long spear-shaft in his hand. With this he rapped sharply for order, then beckoned someone from a further corner of the court.

Against that wall, separated from the men of Knossos, crouched or stood the Greeks. They were all in their native cloaks, the loose, uncut garment of whitish wool caught at the shoulder by a pin. The girl who had just stepped down, having been sold to the head of the clay workers, had shed her outer cloak, and, that all bidders might behold she was sound and strong, stood clad in a short garment of white, very much like the kilt which Inas wore.

Inas looked along the wall. Five of the Greeks had already been sold; eight more awaited the auctioneer's bidding. Theseus only was absent. Inas wondered at that.

PAUSING HERE BEHIND A PILLAR, INAS LOOKED DOWN.

On the floor, at the end of the line, crouched the smallest of the Greek girls, Dité. Her eyes were red and swollen from weeping and, as Inas watched her, she stifled a sob in the folds of her cloak in an attempt to imitate the stoicism of her companions. Such a baby, thought Inas, and such a pity she had ever been sent from home.

Inas, watching, saw a man called from the group and mount the platform. He dropped his cloak and stood, silent, haughtily gazing out over the heads of his bidders. He had been conspicuous in the Bull Ring and should bring a fair price from a good master. But that poor child in the corner . . . Inas stepped down toward the court.

She made her way quietly around the wall and sat down at the end of the line, next to Dité. Tugging at the girl's cloak, she drew her attention and gained a faint, watery smile of recognition.

"Do not fear," she whispered in Greek. "These are good people." She nodded toward the bidders, whose attention was all on the auctioneer. "This is not the slave market, in which anyone may bid. There is the head of the smiths and weapon makers, a fine man with three daughters and a big house. And there is the chief of the rug weavers; he has been my father's friend all my life, and he lives right here in the palace. Almost any of these people would take you to a good home."

One large dark eye peered from behind the cloak, wistfully, wanting to believe. "They told us," sniffed Dité, "that we'd be eaten by the Cretans."

"Stuff and nonsense," snorted Inas. "Eaten! We don't eat humans. Why, they tell us the Greeks do that, so you can see—!"

The little Greek girl giggled, softly, reluctantly, but still a giggle. There, that was better!

The bidding was brisk; for the auctioneer, a man unknown to

Inas, was an excellent salesman. The young Greek was knocked down to a man who was the head of the pottery workers in the palace. None but actual friends of Minos were allowed to bid at this auction. The receipts, which would be high, went to the king but it was considered a privilege, even an honor, to be allowed the purchase of a Greek. Who would come next? Inas wondered. Another of the men probably.

"You next!" ordered the auctioneer and crooked a commanding finger.

Inas looked up, gazed around, bewildered. Why . . . why the man was ordering her—

She got up quietly, stepped to the small platform, mounted it and glanced around. Someone chuckled in the back of the room. Inas dropped her eyes demurely. Of course the salesman was a stranger, he had heard her speaking Greek, she was dressed in white, as were the others, and with a scarf draping the fillet on her hair. What else could he think?

"Here is one of the younger slaves," stated the auctioneer, "sound and well, as are all these girls. A sturdy outdoor girl, as one can tell by her color. She looks clever. Do you speak the tongue?" He meant Cretan.

Inas merely widened her blue eyes at him as though in complete uncomprehension. Someone else snorted. It was Meropes, who, as commander of the Fleet, would be among the honored ones present. The rug weaver came out with a bid.

"Ten gold pieces," he offered. It was surprisingly high for a first bid. Inas felt flattered and sent him a little smile. His eyes crinkled with mirth and he nodded at her to indicate that he too thought the jest a good one.

"Two pieces and a bar of gold," came in a harsh, tight voice from the back of the court. Inas, peering toward the corner, was unable to recognize the speaker, as she stood in a full flood of light and the court seemed dim beyond her. By now the Greeks had caught the point and were watching gravely, and Dité, forgetting her own troubles, was smiling above the fold of her cloak.

The auctioneer held up one of Inas' hands. "See, she is fair and her hands are those of the well-born, not of a toiler in the fields. No doubt she is excellent with the needle—"

Inas, who could not sew a stitch and was the most notorious tomboy in all Knossos, bit her lips. Someone cried, "Three pieces and a bar of gold."

Immediately the harsh voice of the former bidder responded with, "Three bars, I bid."

Inas looked again toward that corner of the room. The shiny, bare skull, that beaked nose? Of course the voice was familiar. It was Kres who had bid against the weaver, and again. What was his object? Surely he was not capable of joining in this mild joke on the auctioneer.

Meropes' voice was once more raised to extend the bid. And again Kres replied with a new offer. The bidding followed with increasing speed, crisp and sharp. The auctioneer was obviously puzzled, but delighted by such evidence of his skill and by the large sum from which he could take his percentage, he urged on the bidding.

Inas was worried. The game had gone far beyond its original intention, and with Kres' introduction into the field she had felt an almost snarling defiance, the hint of an underhanded revenge, that might prove most unhappy for her. If Kres did succeed in buying her, and he was wealthy, Ariadne would stand by her. But there was a law that any free man or woman might sell himself or herself into slavery for a certain time if they wished freedom from want, or needed to work off a debt. No one, in his right mind, would consider this a serious sale, since Inas had been at the first mistaken for a Greek. But Kres might press his rights. And Minos was jealously careful of his reputation of the "Just One."

The bids had now risen to the astounding price of ten bars of gold, three bags of silver. Never had any slave brought such a price; why, it was a small fortune in itself. Inas, feeling a rising panic, choked it back. She wished that Daidalos were here. She must find some way to end this. If she showed her crown per-haps—she had forgotten that it was hidden by the scarf on her head, but it should certainly gain her some privileges.

The last bid had been from Kres. Somewhat reluctant that bid had been. Inas sensed that he was reaching a point beyond which even his hatred for her and her father would not carry him. The man was wealthy but notoriously a miser.

The auctioneer, elated by this strange success, again praised the charms of his wares. "See," he cried, pounding his staff on the dais for emphasis, "see how beautiful is her hair, how firm and strong her ankles, how fine her face."

Strange to hear yourself analyzed, like a mule or a dog for sale. Meropes caught her eye and nodded reassuringly. He too must know the danger, but the father of Kadmos was as wealthy, al-most, as Kres, and never had he been accused of greed or avarice.

Inas felt relieved. It was going to be all right. If necessary, she thought that two or three of her father's friends would band together to bid down the gold worker. And that indeed must have been what happened. She saw word pass between them and then Meropes suddenly raised the bid. "Twenty bars of gold!" he cried in a firm voice.

A gasp ran through the court. "Twenty bars bid for the maid?" For a moment the auctioneer was too stunned to take up the offer, then rallying, he cried, "Am I bid more? Am I bid—" His glance sought out the gold worker. Kres shook his head sourly. That was enough, more would be sheer folly. Sullenly he shouldered his way to the door and passed out.

A breath, almost a sigh of relief, seemed to go through the audience. Inas felt as though chains had been suddenly struck from her wrists and ankles. Now all would be well, since none here would hold her to the sale, and for a small fee the auctioneer would forget the foolish jest . . . if only he would be made to recognize it as a jest. Perhaps . . .

The auctioneer made a gesture, waved Inas down from the steps, indicating that she was to go to Meropes. But Inas, laughing, tossed back the scarf about her hair, showing the gold fillet about her forehead and, bubbling with suppressed laughter and relief, placed her hand on the head of the auctioneer, slightly below her. Her voice rang clear through the court, in the Cretan tongue that all might hear and understand.

"Now, good sirs," she challenged the bidders, "what am I offered for this very excellent auctioneer?"

CHAPTER TWELVE

THE DOOR IN THE LABYRINTH

That had been a close escape! By the time she reached the upper hallway, off the princess's apartments, Inas' heart had ceased its rapid hammering. She paused for a moment outside the doorway and a slave girl coming out with the remains of the morning meal smiled and nodded to her. Inas pushed aside the curtain.

The princess was receiving her stewards. There were two of them; one, the head of the royal treasury, brisk and business-like, who had just reported the monthly sum placed at Ariadne's disposal. Each month Minos appointed an amount to be used for entertainment and for household expenses to be paid into the household coffer. Ariadne, as chief of the housekeeping, was supposed to keep within that sum.

Now she was busy with Kloritoss, the steward of the royal household, a garrulous, plump little person who fancied himself far more efficient than the steward of the royal treasury, but who took an infinity of time to discuss the windy nothings with which he was inflated. Ariadne flashed Inas a mischievous smile as though to beg, "Release me, if you are a loyal subject, from this cataract of words!" But she was patient with him, nevertheless, and listened with apparent attention.

"And the oil which Your Highness has ordered to be opened was received in faulty containers and is no longer of first quality.

We recommend that it be sold in the market for the inferior grade which it is and that—"

"Yes, yes, you are quite right, Kloritoss. And you," she turned to the steward of the royal treasury, "is there more you wish to discuss this morning?" She put her hand to her head as though such a multiplicity of details had been too wearying for the royal head. The treasurer took his hint.

"That is all, Your Highness." He made obeisance and took a swift departure, followed by the gratitude of both Ariadne and Inas.

"Come here," The princess beckoned Inas to sit on a cushion at her feet. "You have news for me?"

But Kloritoss had not yet finished his work of the morning. "And the grain that was received from Thebes, that should soon be ground, and made into flour. If it is so ordered—"

"It is ordered. Indeed it is ordered. I trust you in all these things, Kloritoss." The old steward, beaming, puttered toward the door.

Inas broke into a description of the slave auction and her own part in it. Twice in the course of her tale she was interrupted by the return of Kloritoss. He had bad news, very bad news indeed. It seemed that the octopus, usually so plentiful in Cretan waters, was found no more in the fishermen's nets and the fishermen themselves were becoming strangely superstitious over the failure of this favorite eight-armed delicacy.

"And they say, Your Highness, that the failure of the catches of this symbol of Minos presages some terrible disaster to Crete."

"Oh!" Ariadne burst into delighted laughter. "What nonsense! Has Pharaoh of Egypt lost his throne because the lotus fails to bloom along the Nile? Tell the fishermen to fish farther to the west or to the east, and they will find octopus as before."

"That was wise counsel," commented Inas as the old man, mumbling and beaming, puttered away. "You, who have had no traffic with the fishing fleet—"

"Faugh! One learns at least to read people in this trade of mine and to tell a bold tale. I know not whether the lotuses of Pharaoh have failed or not, and as to the octopus, that is nonsense, Crete is as she has always been and always will be."

Mention of Ariadne's ability to read character had reminded Inas of the Greeks and of Theseus. "They say," she began as one who relates stale news, "that the Greeks attempted to escape."

"When? Where?" Ariadne was all attention. "Tell me."

"Oh, but this is not new. It happened yesterday. Teeta heard it in the morning market." And at the princess's impatient urging, Inas went on to tell what she had heard from Daidalos. "And Father thinks it shameful they were so trapped since, if they had but turned to the right instead of to the left, they would have found a doorway to the river bank."

Ariadne now had hold of Inas' wrist. Never had bringer of news received more flattering attention. "Is he sure? How does he know? Below and to the right you say?" The questions showered from her lips.

"He knows well for when he rebuilt the Labyrinth five years ago he discovered this opening. It is not sealed, he says, but is so hidden in shape and color by the rock that one would never dream it there. He told me because he thought that Minos and his family should know of it, though when he discovered it he did tell the king."

"Oh . . . I . . . wonder." Ariadne plunged her chin into her palm and thought. Inas was quiet. In a moment the princess looked up and her expression changed. "Yes, Kloritoss, what is it now?"

"The Greek slaves? Your Highness had given orders that one Theseus was to be purchased for the summer palace. But Minos has commanded that he is not yet to be freed from the prison."

"Princess," Inas put a hesitating hand onto the other's arm, "a slight favor, if it is possible."

"Yes, indeed. What is it?"

"The little Greek girl, Dité, of whom I told you. If she could be purchased, to be among the princess's own slaves?"

"Yes," Ariadne was indifferent, but kind. "You hear, Kloritoss? Find this girl named . . . Dité? Find her and if she has not already been sold buy her. If she belongs to another see if she can be repurchased for me."

But Kloritoss still lingered, to protest. "These Greeks, they are good on the farms, as shepherds and tenders of mules, and the women for farm work, but for the household they are clumsy and idle and dishonest."

The opposition was sufficient to rouse Ariadne's stubbornness. "Go!" she cried imperiously, stamping her small brown foot. "Purchase the maiden and bring her here. Go!"

Then as Kloritoss scuttled through the doorway she turned to grin ruefully at a startled Inas. "There, that is the only way to rid oneself of that old woman in the garments of a man! For half a day I can put up with his chatterings, then I turn sour as cream in a thunderstorm. Oh—!" she drew a great sigh of relief and stretched her arms toward the ceiling. "Now come, Inas, and tell me more of this Greek."

"Dité?" asked Inas with apparent innocence.

"No, stupid one, of this Theseus."

CHAPTER THIRTEEN

A JAR OF HONEY

Although Daidalos had taken his summons to the palace as of no great importance, Inas was more concerned than she cared to show. Certain small nothings, a whisper there, a glance here, the ceasing of talk among Ariadne's maidens when Inas approached, as though they had been discussing her, the warnings of Glos, Kadmos' concern, all these were little things, but were beginning to pile into something much greater.

"But, Father, where should we go if we left Crete?" she worried.

Daidalos made a little gesture of impatience and went on with the work he had already started when Inas entered his workshop. A wooden wheel, very wide, was held on his work-bench by a loop of string which passed down through the bench and ended in a stirrup held beneath his foot. With a delicate bronze chisel, which he whetted constantly on a piece of smooth black stone, and a light wooden mallet Daidalos was cutting into the broad smooth face of the wheel, or roller. Releasing the weight with his foot, he turned the roller slightly, showing that only a small strip of it remained uncarved.

Inas persisted. "Where, Father?" she begged again.

"There are many places," he assured her, "if departure from Crete became indeed a necessity. My name is not unknown, and kings of many lands, both far and near, have offered me gold and fame if I would advise them as to the strengthening of their city walls, the training or arming of their soldiers, the building of their ships—all matters which, except for Crete herself, do not concern me. Though . . ." he seemed to muse aloud, "if ever I left these shores—"

"But you said we need not leave," Inas reminded him.

"No, we need not leave. Minos but warned me, reminded me of the ignorance of the people, a fact I had not quite forgotten." His tone was ironical. "And that such experiments as I had been making must either cease or be covered with greater secrecy."

He finished carving the last strip of the roller, and having released the holding strap, held the carved piece vaguely and indecisively in his hand. He gazed for a moment about the workshop, then dampened his fingers in a small dish of water and with ready inventiveness rubbed them across the sooty top of the charcoal support over which he did the heating necessary for his experiments. Absently, it seemed to Inas, he smeared the clean white wood of the roller, over and over, with the soot. Not until he had repeated the action several times did she realize that it was intentional.

"You were right," he continued, "to persuade me to move to the cave of the cliffs, though at the time I felt discovery was unimportant. Now I have refused to leave Crete, because of this imagined danger, unless Minos should pass a definite decree of exile. In that case, of course, I should feel that my loyalty and my inventions might be transferred to strengthen another king and another country."

Inas felt slightly relieved. She could imagine living nowhere but in Crete, in Knossos. Still, if the king were concerned over the safety of Daidalos . . .

"Then we are staying?" she asked.

Daidalos nodded vaguely. His left hand drew the light cloth of his tunic smoothly over his thigh, his right hand rolled the sooted roller down its length. There, upon the cloth appeared a simple pattern of a flying fish, repeated twice in full and half again.

"Swifter than embroidery," he commented of the result. "Of course the roller might also be cut with symbols of writing, but who would wish the same symbols, endlessly repeated?"

In the morning, very early and before daylight Daidalos departed for the caves to test the new theory regarding flight against the wind. None knew of his departure save Inas and Teeta. To the remainder of the household he was still in his workshop, intent on some task and not to be disturbed.

Inas was planning to follow him in a day or two. She was still greatly concerned over the loss of Ariadne's ring, and did not wish to leave Knossos till she had found and returned it to the princess.

It would be better not to ask Teeta outright about the ring. If the old woman had taken it, put it away for safekeeping, she would, reminded of it in some way, be sure to mention the fact. Impossible that she had stolen it, as impossible as accusing an immediate member of Inas' family! But how to lead up to the subject?

Inas, playing with Sizi in her lap while she dangled her long legs from the railing, considered the matter. Sizi nipped at her finger, Inas drew it away. What sharp little teeth the kitten had, and what a rough, pink little tongue!

"Oh, hum!" she yawned openly. "With Father away, life will be quieter here, and now that Kadmos has gone fishing—"

Teeta, busy with distaff and hank of rosy dyed yarn, gave a derisive sniff. "When I was a girl—" she commenced.

"Oh, yes, and I too will tell my children the same tale. But with the Bull Ring over—" Inas waited. Would the mention of Kadmos, or of a ring, even the Bull Ring, bring a flicker of remembrance of that other ring?

Teeta twirled the spindle whorl between long, flattened yellow finger and thumb, but there was no quiver of the blue ear drops, the usual index of inner emotion. Inas sighed again. Neither "Kadmos" nor "ring" had done the trick. Now Sizi . . . she eyed the kitten with speculative gaze. But the ring did not glitter, had neither pleasant smell nor flavor to attract a small cat's curiosity. Unlikely that he would play with it, though he might have patted the cover from the box, and pawed the contents which could have rolled into a corner of the room. Inas had searched high and low but there was no small crevice where the ring could have fallen to remain hidden.

Mufu appeared in the doorway, his black face beaming with unconcealed interest, his kinky locks standing straight out, as though newly washed. Usually they lay quite flat to his head with oil and much patting. He muttered a message to the Egyptian; someone was outside with a package to be delivered. Teeta, still spinning, rose and departed to answer the summons. Inas was left with Mufu and the kitten. Which of these might be the culprit?

Sizi scrabbled frantically for foothold on the rail, then half falling to the floor, scuttled for Mufu's bare toes. The boy grinned and bent to pick him up. Inas' eyes narrowed with speculation.

Today her own hair was twisted about Kadmos' gift, the gold and crystal pin. Now she drew it out suddenly with a little exclamation of apparent fright. "Oh, the pin nearly touched my head!" she cried.

Mufu, startled, looked his curiosity.

"Don't you know," explained Inas dramatically, "that if gold touches your head it will burn right through to your brains? It's really very dangerous to wear gold near the head."

Mufu's eyes grew enormous with sudden fright and with a shriek he began clutching frantic fingers through his kinky mane. Watching with amusement, Inas saw something fall from his hands and go bouncing and skipping across the flat stones of the floor. Mufu, still with hands to head, fled screeching from the room.

Inas dropped limply from the railing and with tears of laughter streaming down her cheeks sank to the floor. She was still holding her aching sides when Teeta returned, bearing a jar in her hand.

"What is the matter with Mufu?" she asked, frowning.

Inas shook her head. "Just a small joke I played on him. It was of no great importance. I dropped something here . . ." On her knees, she fumbled for the ring, picked it up. It was the ring she had been seeking, but the pure soft gold had been badly dented from the fall. The little deer now danced on wavering legs, the circle was bent and difficult to fit over the finger. Inas regarded it with dismay. There was no question, the ring must be repaired before it could be returned to the princess. She must ask her father's assistance, get him to recommend a gold worker clever enough to repair the damage. Or perhaps Daidalos himself . . . yes, that might be better. Her father had wonderful skill with almost any tool.

Teeta's inquiring eyes were upon her. Inas, who did not wish to be questioned, dropped the ring for safekeeping into the little leather bag at her belt. Tomorrow she would go to the cliffs, ask Daidalos to repair the ring and return it, at last, to the princess.

She turned her attention to Teeta. "What have you—a message from the king?" she asked. The beautiful little jar with its sprawling octopus decoration was just such a priceless gift as Minos always sent with his messengers.

Teeta shook her head. "No message, only this." She set the jar on a shelf and began to spin again.

"Strange." Inas rose to examine it. The jar was gracefully modeled, of some black ware made abroad but decorated at the palace workshops. Over its wide mouth was a cover of vellum held tightly in place by a twist of bright thread. The thread was sealed, as were all Minos' gifts, with his personal signet, two goddesses offering sacrifice before a sacred pillar.

Inas looked inquiringly at the Egyptian. "Let us open and see what it is," she suggested. "Father will not care. Doubtless it is some strange sweet that in any case he would share with us."

Teeta grunted, saying neither aye nor nay. Inas took the knife from the sheath at her belt. Attracted by the movement of the weapon, Sizi came scuttling across the floor. Inas picked up the jar and gathering the kitten into her lap sat down, cross-legged on the floor, to cut the cord about the vellum.

The seal tinkled on the floor. Inas raised the lid and peered within.

"Oh . . . oh, honey!" She plunged a forefinger into the jar, withdrew it, dripping with a sticky mass of sugared honey, delicious to the nostrils, doubtless as delectable to the tongue.

Teeta clucked reprovingly. "That is no way to eat," she chided. "Wait and I will bring a spoon." She jumped up and departed, still spinning. Inas chuckled.

"Teeta disapproves of us, Sizi. Honey. Do you like the taste?"

For the little cat was licking at the extended finger with half shut eyes and little ecstatic purrs of pleasure. "Greedy," Inas scolded the kitten. "Now I shall have to wait till I have the spoon and a proper dish. Then you may have more if you like it, though I cannot believe that the king's honey is a proper food for little cats, even sacred cats."

As Teeta returned with a spoon and a dish Inas rose, setting the kitten down. Inas spooned out a lump of the honey and brought it beneath Teeta's nose. "Smells delightful, doesn't it? Taste it."

The Egyptian shook her head, pushing the dish away with an impatient hand. "Careful, you will drop stickiness on my yarn. Taste it yourself."

But the spoon went clattering to the dish. Inas uttered a little scream. "Teeta! Look at the kitten!"

Sizi lay on his side, his furry little legs convulsively twitching, his mouth open and gasping. Even as the girl crossed the floor to him, he lay still. She bent and touched him with a gentle hand, then looked up at the Egyptian, who stood above her.

"Dead!" she stated flatly. Their eyes met in startled horror. A long moment passed before Teeta spoke; then in a hoarse voice she said: "The honey. Wash it from your hand!"

Yes, that was it. The honey. With shaking knees Inas went swiftly to find water and wood ashes with which to scour her fingers. Strange how sweet, almost sickish now, the honey scent. She wiped her hands vigorously on a cloth, took the cloth to the fire, dropped it in and watched it smolder to ashes, then returned to Teeta.

The old woman still stood where Inas had left her, gazing down at the kitten. For the moment too concerned even to mourn for the little beast, Inas crossed to the jar. Without touching it she examined the vellum cover, picked up the wax that had sealed it.

"Who brought this, Teeta?" she asked.

Teeta shook her head. "I do not know the man. He said there was no message, and though it seemed strange I thought that the message might follow. It is the king's seal?"

Yes, there was no question about the seal. Who could have access to such a seal, or even to a perfect copy of it? Who, that hated this household?

"For Daidalos," the messenger had said. No one had known of Daidalos' departure. Among his many enemies who was there with so deadly a hatred as to plan his death thus, with a jar of poisoned honey?

"Kres, the gold worker." Involuntarily Inas spoke aloud. Teeta clicked terse assent with her tongue.

"Daidalos must be told, must be warned of this." Inas continued to think aloud. "Tonight before sundown I will start for the cliff. I had thought to go anyway and this has decided me. If anything comes during my absence, keep it. Keep secret also my departure and if any ask for Daidalos, say that he is busy on a commission for the king and must not be disturbed."

Teeta nodded. "Yes, that is good," she agreed.

"Moreover, bury Sizi beneath the stones of the yard." For a moment her voice choked, then she added firmly, "And the honey, bury that also."

CHAPTER FOURTEEN

SEA FLIGHT

She might have guessed, Inas told herself, that her father would take it like that. His first question, once she had completed her account of the poisoned honey, was, "Where then is this honey?"

"I directed Teeta to bury it. It seemed unwise to leave it anywhere in the household. Do you agree?"

"Quite wise." Daidalos paused with a little skeptical smile. "If indeed the honey was poisoned."

Inas nearly stamped her foot with annoyance. "But, Father—the kitten—!"

"Of what other dish had your little cat eaten this morning?" he asked reasonably.

"Why—" Inas paused to consider. "Goat's milk. Meat or fish possibly. I do not know. Teeta fed him often."

"Perhaps," he suggested, "even something he ate outside our household. Oh, my dear child!" He raised his hand in protest. "I do not mean to say that it is not all quite possible. The gold worker has just cause to hate me, even to wish to destroy me. Our aims and ambitions have always been along different roads. Indeed there is little doubt that he might have sent the honey, or that the dish may have been poisoned."

"May, indeed!" snorted Inas, in what was a fair imitation of Teeta herself. "Oh, Father," she crossed the cave to put her arm around him, "only be careful, more careful than ever, in the future, I do beg of you."

Daidalos patted her shoulder but said nothing.

"There is one other thing." Inas wondered if she would get a scolding for this. "Ariadne's ring." She showed him where the soft gold had been twisted and bent as it was thrown by the terrified Mufu. "Can that be mended?" she asked, pointing to the distorted legs of the little deer. "I mean, can you do it?"

Daidalos examined it silently, asking no questions, though he must have recognized it as the seal of the princess. Yes, it could be mended, he told Inas, and yes, he could do it. "But not here. I shall need the tools and a good fire, such as I have in town. Show it to me again in a few days and I will make it right again. And now suppose you try the wings. I have already relaced and tested them."

Inas had come from town on the white mule, Ion, riding first along the dusty main road, then turning off on a tiny, little-traveled way and at last, with the mule left at the house of a friendly fisherman on the cliff, making the remainder of the trip on foot.

Once, long ago, these caves along the cliffs had been dwellings for the poorer fishermen. Now they were deserted, ownerless, and no one ever visited them save perhaps a stray goat-herd or a small boy. If Daidalos chose to come here, well, he was known to be a harmless man, though a strange one, and country-folk pride themselves on minding their own business. It is in cities and small towns that gossip rises, to spread like a low poisonous fog on a windless day.

The cave was comfortable, dry, and airy. One side had been partly walled in, with two small windows opening onto a wide grass-covered meadow that ran down to another cliff above the sea. These two steep steps, with the grassy ground between was what made the place so safe, so perfect for Daidalos' experiments. That and the keen sea wind which was blowing today.

Inas, inspecting the place again with its possibilities for flight in mind, wondered if it would be possible to drop from the second cliff into the water beneath. The salty breeze was straight from the northeast. If her theory was correct, that she could glide better against the wind than with it, then with any luck she should land some distance out on the water, escaping the rocks below. Even if she failed, the wings would break her fall.

She returned to the cave for her wings and picked her way to a smooth spot, well back from the cliff's edge, that she might have a short run before taking off. Her father had remained in the cave. Save for the squeal of the gulls above her, seeming to laugh at these poor human attempts to fly, and the soft rush of wind through the tall grass the sunlit place was silent and deserted. Best, however, to look over and see where she might land. She put down the wings, anchored them with a convenient stone and walked to the edge.

Below her the rock sheered away swiftly for a space, then sloped gradually to the deep blue water. A small, solitary boat, painted blue, lay gently rocking almost beneath her. Inas gave a little exclamation and backed away from the edge. With just her head above the rocks she examined the boat more closely. Its sail was furled, the stone anchors out at either end and at the stern a single figure crouched, intent on its fishing lines. But by the giant eye and the long sea raven's beak painted on the bow, Inas recognized it, and recognized too, though she could not see the face, the crouching figure that did not look up. She laughed and turned back toward her wings. This was going to startle Kadmos.

Her hair blew against her face in banners of bright color, her short, full trousers clung close to her body, her sash rippled like a flag before her and when she lifted the wings she found them difficult to adjust, so strong and steady was the pull of the wind. She gave a final glance around her. Still no one in sight; then she poised, wind buffeted, before making the run toward the edge. For just a moment Inas felt a tug of fear, but the exhilaration of the lifting wings as the wind caught her and the need for concentration drowned her emotion. Her feet left the earth. She was out, out over the cliff.

She had counted on a steep angle of landing, as steep perhaps as a stairway, even perhaps like a steep hill. But the wind was deceitful. Though she tipped her body and tried to shorten her flight by changing her weight and tilting the wings, she was carried on. Out the wind carried her; over with a rush that swept her many boat lengths from the shore, then down, down in a slow delicious glide. This was the best of all.

The *Sea Raven* was far behind, but as she tilted the glider with the weight of her body, banked to lessen her distance from the shore, she swung round facing the rocks again. She saw the stone anchors come up swiftly, first in the stern, then in the bow, and the hurrying figure seize the long steering pole in the stern and start rapidly toward her through the blue water.

By then she was down, gently subsiding on the waves, the glider catching enough air beneath the linen to hold her for some time bouyant on the water. No matter if it had not. Inas could have reached the shore by swimming. She closed her eyes a moment to shut out the dazzle of light, to enjoy fully this delightful culmination of her flight. Then opening them, chuckled as she watched the *Raven* approach.

It moved swiftly, for so heavy a boat. The boy in the stern poled skillfully, with strength and firmness. Inas, paddling with her hands while she kicked gently with her feet, made some progress toward the boat. The boy's whole attention seemed, for the moment, on his pole, Inas' on the speed of his approach, so that she was totally unprepared for his next movement.

With a strong twist of his pole that shot the craft forward in a final spurt, Kadmos dropped his oar and snatched up his spear. Before Inas gathered his intent, he was standing in the prow, scarcely a bowshot away, pointing the weapon directly at the strange, winged creature on the water. Then with a sudden realization that the glare on the water, combined with the strangeness of her descent, could have given him a completely mistaken idea of who and what she was, Inas called out sharply:

"Hold your weapon, O swift warrior. I am human and a Cretan!"

Then she burst into laughter at the expression on his face. Still half doubting, Kadmos slowly lowered his arm till the bronze-tipped spear rested on the gunwale, but did not entirely relinquish it until Inas had removed her arms from the glider, dived beneath and come up, dragging it behind her. Then with a deep

HOLD YOUR WEAPON, O SWIFT WARRIOR —
I AM HUMAN AND A CRETAN!

frown cleaving his brows he reached a hand to haul her over the side of the boat. Of late, Kadmos always seemed to be dragging her into boats.

Inas expected a scolding, but wished to defer the storm as long as possible. "I would save the wings," she cried. "Wait—they will dry in the sun and the wood is not yet soaked enough to warp."

Kadmos had been silently willing to help her aboard, but he would lend no hand in salvaging the winged creature. He let her recover the glider unaided. It was difficult, for the wings were sodden, the gunwale was high, and the wind caught beneath the linen, twisting the frame as though it were diabolically alive.

Finally the glider lay across the end of the boat, propped evenly, drying in the hot sun. Dripping with sea-water, Inas prolonged the wringing of her hair which served as a convenient curtain before her face. Between its strands she could see Kadmos eye the wings dubiously, his frown slowly relaxing. At last, having put it off as long as she dared, she flung her wet locks over her shoulder and turned to face him.

"I thought you were some strange bird," Kadmos explained slowly. "A moment more, had you not called when you did, and I would have speared you and taken you to show the king."

"Did you not see me sail from the cliff?" asked Inas, astonished.

Kadmos' hand was on the pole again; he began to edge the boat back toward the shore. "Your shadow crossed the water before me, but when I looked up, the light was so bright I could see nothing but giant wings against the sky." He still spoke slowly, glancing sideways at the drying glider.

Inas was impatient. "The wings are, after all, no more mysterious or frightening than the sails of your boat," she told him. "Someday you too may use them." And as the boy murmured, "The gods forbid!" she laughed and shrugged.

"See, there is Father now." She pointed toward the cliff which they were approaching. Above the upper rock, like a huge and awkward gull, appeared Daidalos with his wings. For a moment he paused, silhouetted against the sky, swung his body to tilt the wings, then planed downward toward the meadow, and was lost behind the edge of the lower cliff. In a moment he appeared again, this time without the glider, and seemed to be looking for Inas. The girl raised her hands to her mouth and called out to him. Daidalos looked downward, seemed to catch sight of the boat and waved an arm in recognition. Inas sighed and sat down.

"Do not be angry with me, Kadmos," she begged, returning to the subject of the glider. "Each child must have his toy. Yours is the sea, perhaps, but ours is the air."

Kadmos' anger seemed to have vanished, dissolved in his concern for her and her father. "It is no wonder that Daidalos is accused of black magic," he said gravely. "Had one or two fisher boats been here, had others seen you land, like a bird, on the water, then Minos himself could not have saved you and your father from the charge of witch-craft."

"Oh, Kadmos," she said impatiently, "I am always careful. I only risked such a landing because I recognized you and your *Sea Raven*. And the cliff itself is completely deserted now."

"And your father, did he look first to see if any fisher boats were in sight?" Kadmos reminded her. Inas was silent. That was true. Daidalos had been cautious enough in the beginning, but now he was so accustomed to the idea of the wings that he no longer considered them as either terrible or strange. He was too concerned with improving his invention.

The pole made a little, widening ripple in the dark water, there was a soft sucking as waves ran gently in and out between the rocks along the shore. It was pleasantly cool here, under the lee of the cliff. Inas looked up along its steep rocky sides. Yes, it had been dangerous but it was worth it.

The wings would be difficult to carry back without tearing. The cloth and cord were dry now, though entangled with seaweed, but the wood was still too wet for flying. It would be wiser perhaps to loosen the cord and roll the cloth around the wooden frame. She bent silently to her work.

Kadmos dropped his anchor overboard at the stern and came toward her. "Let me help you with that. I am no longer frightened, like a silly sheep." He knelt beside her. "Or leave the wings here. Tonight I will bring them back to you in the cave."

Inas made room for him. "Help me now," she said, "and I will promise to fly no more—today."

CHAPTER FIFTEEN

A BLACK THREAD

That day the wind had been favorable to the wings but the same night it changed. For two days Inas hung restlessly about the cave, tried to cook for her father, who was a far better cook than she, tried to mend a garment for him, and spent hours gazing restlessly from the doorway while flying spume was flung from the great breakers that broke against the cliff. This was one of Crete's periodical wind-storms. It might clear tomorrow; it might last six or seven days.

Twice Kadmos fought his way along the upper cliff, through wind and blown rain, down the path to the cave, but on the third day he came to say that his fishing was spoiled and he was returning to Knossos. He had heard rumors of a strange black boar, a huge, raging beast that was destoying crops, menacing flocks and their herders in a place not far from the mountain where Glos had his hut.

Daidalos scoffed at the story: "That is not boar country. It is too high and rocky and dry. Someone has probably seen a large black ram, or the boar is in the land to the north, not where Glos lives," he suggested.

Kadmos departed late that afternoon for the city. Next day, the fourth of her stay in the cave, Daidalos suggested that Inas also return to Knossos.

"You are too young to spend your time in contemplation through an open window," he remarked dryly. "Besides, I have further experiments to make, and, while you are often of great assistance, when I wish merely to think—"

"I know, you can do it better without me," Inas agreed good-naturedly. "Yes, I will return to Knossos for a few days till the storm has ceased." And late that afternoon she struggled through the wind up the meadow to the little hut where Ion was tethered.

It would be nice to be back in Knossos, although it was always pleasant to get away to the rough life of a shepherd's hut, where goat's milk and cheese and black bread were heavenly food because of the appetite gained by long hours spent in the open chasing the black bulls, spearing fish, or just racing across open pasture. But court life was interesting too. Inas was too much a young girl, too pretty, and too fond of clothes and jewels, of fans and scented gloves, and the delicious foods and music of court life, not to enjoy her visits to the palace and their stimulating contrast to the other side of her life.

But on this return she found the Knossos house just a little sad and lonely without Sizi. Inas had not realized that she would miss the kitten as much as this; his funny endearing little purr, his dancing steps, and his pretended fright with fluffed-out tail at a blown feather or flapping curtain.

"Perhaps," Teeta suggested when she saw the girl's depression, "perhaps the princess may have another kitten she will give you."

"I don't think I can ever replace Sizi," Inas' tone was mournful, but Teeta uttered the snort that did duty with her for laughter.

"Nonsense! One kitten is very like another kitten. Each will play with its tail, drink milk, eat fish, and get under foot. Now away with you to the palace! Ariadne will be glad of your return, and I shall not be sorry to rid myself of your mournful face for a time."

Feeling comically like a small chicken that had been shooed out of the way, Inas went to prepare herself for a visit to the palace. She put on her finest robe, the color of the wild pink geranium, with its high collar that rose behind her beribboned head. She put on sandals of fine embroidered leather; and for covering, since even here in the city the wind was strong and cold, a long cloak of blue-dyed Egyptian weave.

Yes, Teeta was wise, she thought, as she made her way toward the palace. Always something amusing happened where Ariadne held court. Gossips of the town, musicians, mountebanks, traders, all came to her apartments and were welcomed for the diversity of tales they told, of wares they displayed, or of tricks they performed.

Inas found the princess carding wool on the terrace and alone except for her little blue African monkey. The chattering girls were crowded over some game in the light-well room beyond.

The princess looked up with a smile of welcome. "Come, sit beside me and tell me the news of the city." She patted the cushioned step on which she sat. "Child, you have hurried and are very warm. Here, take this fan. I am glad you are back but you may wish to ride out to the hunt this evening."

Inas fanned swiftly, sending a little breeze through the princess's curls. "That is good wool," she said and paused to feel it between experimental finger and thumb.

Ariadne nodded. "Yes, it is good. It should take the dye well. Where have you been?"

"Just down to the shore." Inas shrugged away the question. "Father was there and I went to accompany him. What is this hunt you speak of?"

"It is to kill a great black boar, such a boar as has seldom been seen in Crete. You should know of it, since it is on your father's property. Has he not fields on the slope of Mount Iuctus?"

"A boar? There?" Inas dropped her fan and gazed thoughtfully at the further wall of the light-well, visible through the uncurtained doorway. A group of laughing dancers decorated the wall but she did not see the dancers. She was seeing the little shepherd's hut on the mountainside and wondering why Glos had sent no word of this boar to her father. "I should like to go," she decided suddenly. "May I go, then, with you?"

Ariadne bent closer over the carding, pulling the sharp wire-toothed comb toward her, dropping the carded wool into the bright rush basket at her side. The monkey scuttled across the terrace, and the princess, half laughing, pushed him away, then stooped to cover the basket from his prying paws. When she straightened again she seemed to have forgotten the question for she said, "There will be plenty of room. Father commanded that the big tents be sent out this morning and I know Deukalion wishes to go also; he has a new spear to try."

"Shall I come here then and travel out with you?" Inas repeated her question, absently pulling the monkey's tail; then, glancing sideways quickly, was amazed to see Ariadne's face bright with blushes.

"I . . . I . . ." stammered the other. How strange to see the princess confused! Inas had a sudden inspiration. "Princess, you stay behind to see this Greek!"

"Hush!" Ariadne spoke sharply and put a slim hand over the girl's mouth, then looked across to the light-well. But the noise about the game, tossing dice in a bowl, was sufficient to cover their conversation.

"No one can hear us," Inas reassured her. But what could Ariadne wish with the Greek? Perhaps a talk with him might be good for her, show her how stupid he really was. Did she then wish Inas to act as an interpreter? All sorts of strange thoughts momentarily chased the other worry from her mind.

Ariadne seemed to make a decision. "I can trust you?" she stated rather than questioned, and at Inas' brisk nod continued: "I want to release him, this Theseus. When the court has gone I shall stay behind on some pretense . . . Oh, only for a few hours, but many of the guards will accompany the hunting party. And now that the other Greeks are sold, there is no guard, I have discovered, at any save the outer door. Then, on the excuse that there is no one near me to send, I shall despatch the soldier on some errand and so give the Greek his opportunity to escape."

"But he is a marked man." Inas was aghast over this mad idea. "He cannot speak our tongue. He could not go the length of five houses, with his great height, his tangled mop of hair, without being noted, since all saw and knew him in the Bull Ring. And he has no friends to escape to; he could never get away from the island."

Ariadne's foot tapped in irritation. "Oh, how foolish you are! I have already thought of such things, planned them carefully.

I will not tell you all, since if the plan should fail it is wiser that I alone know it. But one thing you, and only you, can do for me." She leaned nearer, the carding comb idle in her lap, her voice sunk to a whisper. "Once you spoke of a door in the north corridor, a hidden door in the stone that would open if it were pushed. Can you take word of that secret door to the Greek, show him the way . . . or, no," her eyes fell on the wool in her lap, "better still, put a thread to lead from his prison to this stone that slides. In that way, once he is free of his prison—and I shall see to that—he can escape through the darkness down the path to the river."

Inas looked at her in astonishment. Certainly the princess had put much thought on this rescue of a strange Greek slave. "But how shall I get this message to Theseus?" she asked, in reality seeking a manner of escape from the unwelcome task.

Ariadne's eyes wandered through the group of girls in the room beyond the terrace. "Dité," she commanded.

So the princess had purchased Dité? How pretty the child was with her fluffy hair, the color of wet brown bark, and her great pansy-dark eyes. Inas, who had only seen the little Greek huddled forlornly in her shabby, weather-stained cloak, now put out a hand of welcome. Why, the child was beautiful! With bright color in her cheeks, her hair no longer matted and unkempt but in long ringlets to her waist, she was an altogether different person from the poor little creature Inas had first seen in the palace prison.

Dité murmured a greeting in the Greek tongue, then at Ariadne's chiding glance, stammered the same in broken Cretan.

"I have already given out that Dité is the sister of Theseus," the princess continued with her plot. "So it will be a matter of no great comment if, under your care, she has my consent to visit him in his prison. As for the thread, here, take this yarn—" She picked a ball of black woolen thread from the basket at her feet, then turned at the entrance of a maiden.

"Hana? What is it?"

"Princess, there is a diviner here, who would tell your fortune in the dark liquid."

Ariadne checked a slight movement of impatience. Yes, that was amusing. Yes, she would see the creature, and as the girl turned to summon the sorcerer the princess murmured, "Under cover of this make your departure, Inas. Then return with a report to me. Or, if that seems not wise, send Dité with just a word, 'Well' or 'Ill.'"

With mind divided between concern for the princess and this strange tale of the boar on her father's land, Inas rose to go. Kadmos also had spoken of that boar. What could it mean?

The diviner was a shriveled little man, wrinkled as a toad, bald as a vulture, with red-rimmed eyes staring behind heavy lashless lids. His garb was a nondescript huddle of flapping leather ends and tattered rags bound together with bits of string and rawhide thongs, and a dozen bracelets of some dark metal clanked on ankles and wrists as he moved forward.

Mouthing a toothless, grinning salutation he obeyed the princess's gesture and squatted on the floor some distance away. The maids took seats along the wall or stood waiting with interest but did not crowd near. Indeed, the man was unpleasantly dirty.

"Can you foretell the future truly?" asked Ariadne.

Inas nodded toward Dité and meeting her in the doorway murmured in their common tongue, "Go, I will join you outside and will explain the errand there."

The old one chuckled. "Yes, yes, I can tell what the Fates have spun for you. In the dark liquid here, all is as plain as a happening in the morning's market. See, I will tell your future, kind princess."

"Not mine, not yet." The princess commanded. "Tell . . ." she looked about her, then nodded mischievously toward Inas. "Tell *her* future." Inas turned back with some impatience. Any other time, but not . . .

From some recess of his ragged garments the old man dug up a small, dirt-incrusted bottle and removing the wooden stopper, shook it once or twice against his thumb, then poured a thin dark liquid into one stained palm. Inas thought it was probably the black of the cuttlefish, often used by the palace artisans. He set the bottle beside him on the floor, then folding the other hand beneath the one that held the liquid and bending close above it, he began to weave backward and forward while he mumbled a tuneless little song. No one else stirred.

"I see . . . I see . . ." he began.

With parted lips Inas waited. What would he see for her?

"A long, long journey. Two, three, four such journeys. Smoke and flame against a midnight sky, and the cries of women wailing for their dead." He paused. The place was very still. Someone stirred with a soft rustle of garments and a bee blundered among the roses that bloomed along the terrace wall.

"A small, small boat on a sunny sea, a youth and a maiden sailing . . . They land at Greece."

"That was foolish," thought Inas. "Who would go to Greece in a little boat? And how did he know it was Greece?"

As if he had heard her unspoken query he continued: "Tall houses, square and of logs, and strange people in long cloaks sprawl about a fire. And the princess rises to meet you there. That is all." He stopped rocking and blinked rapidly as though he had just awakened from a sleep.

Inas glanced at Ariadne, whose brown eyes were wide and staring, her cheeks scarlet. "The 'princess' did you say, old man? Tell me, tell me what the dark future holds for me?" She seemed to have forgotten her former disdain of the diviner.

He chuckled weirdly, stirred the mess in his palm with a murky forefinger and again bent to peer nearsightedly into the small black pool. A moment he rocked silently, then the voice came again. "I see a dark thread that leads through darkness, then an opening in the rock, and a boat on water and long days on the sea. The princess is the one in that boat, and the other . . . a tall man, mighty as a pine . . ."

Inas gasped . . . "Above laurels . . ." but no one heard her. That was the phrase the princess herself had used. She was afraid of this. She would listen no more. It was not right, the gods would be angry if one peered thus into the future. She slid from the room.

Only when she encountered Dité in the corridor did she remember Ariadne's errand. It must be done, but the thread, where was that? Reluctantly she turned back, but the old man was silent, still peering; the princess was absorbed in what was to follow. Inas spoke across the width of the terrace.

"Princess? The yarn you would have me match?" For a moment Ariadne regarded her blankly, then, seeming to recollect, picked up the little ball of black thread and tossed it across to her. Inas caught it and hurried out.

With Dité pattering at her heels she almost ran down the corridor, but at the end of the hallway she paused a moment to explain to the child. The princess wished to help Theseus because she felt sorry for the Greeks. Inas knew of a way out of the prison and she was to put the thread in such a way as to lead Theseus to it. If it were possible then Dité was to say, "All is well," when she returned to the princess. If something happened, if, for instance, a guard interfered, then Dité would take back, "All is not well," and the princess must make another plan. Did she understand?

Dité nodded vigorously. Yes, that was indeed simple.

It proved also amazingly simple to execute. Perhaps the guards had gone with the boar hunt, or perhaps it was assumed that a single Greek slave, unarmed, needed no more than a single Cretan soldier to guard him. With a stammered and vague tale of Dité's relationship to the prisoner, Inas was allowed to pass down the Labyrinth toward his cell. At the last corridor Inas told the child to wait for her and went on alone.

First she must find the door in the stone. Without stopping she hurried past Theseus' barred door, came to the end of the passage, made the final turn and met a blank wall. This was what she expected. It smelled dankly of dark earth and mold and was black as a pocket. Dité had been told to cough if she heard anyone coming.

Inas paused a moment to listen, then felt along the stone at the end. To the touch it was all one solid rock, without seam or fissure. She hated this business anyway. It seemed strangely disloyal to her father, even to Crete, but the princess had commanded it, and if Theseus could escape and leave no trace, then no one would be to blame and no one would be harmed.

Ah, a crack in the stone! Her fingers found it and groped along, following. She shoved with all her weight, here, there, and the stone seemed to shift, ever so slightly. Then at the bottom, where the wall met the floor, she saw a faint thread of light. She shoved again.

Far off, down the bend of the corridor, someone coughed. Inas took her weight off the stone. The line faded, almost disappeared. But in that instant she slipped the end of her little black

TO THE TOUCH IT WAS ALL ONE SOLID ROCK
WITHOUT SEAM OR FISSURE

ball of yarn into the crack. The stone closed on it, holding it firmly. She turned, and unwinding the thread as she ran, raced down the corridor of the Labyrinth.

Voices beyond: Dité in stammering conversation with the guard who, though he understood no word of Greek, knew a pretty slave girl when he saw one. Inas thrust the ball of yarn through the bars of Theseus' cell. Someone stirred vaguely against the dim light. She must hurry.

"Quick," she panted, "take the thread and hide it. It will lead you to freedom. Press where the thread enters the stone. The rock will open and you will find a boat at the foot of the hill. The princess has promised that. Here is the guard. Farewell."

She rushed on, to join Dité. At the foot of the steps to Ariadne's apartments Inas told the child. "Say to the princess that all is well. And tell her secretly." She gave the little Greek a pat of affection and left her.

Now at last Inas felt free to consider her own concerns. It was late, almost twilight, and though the sky was light outside, the halls were full of gathering shadows. What was this strange tale of a big black boar? "Near your father's place, at the foot of the mountain," and Kadmos also had heard such a story. Inas wished that Daidalos were here. Surely there was no boar, and if no boar, what then? Who could have reason to bring Minos and his court to land belonging to Daidalos?

She hastened down the steps of the palace, the sunset full in her face. Then she stopped short. The glider! It was still in the cave above the valley of the wings, the glider she herself had made and painted with the head of a bird and decorated with bright feathers. Glos had warned them, her father and herself, that the wings were no longer safe there.

Who would wish to lead Minos and his court to discover the wings . . . who but the gold worker, Kres?

Inas almost raced down the path toward the Knossos house where Ion was tethered.

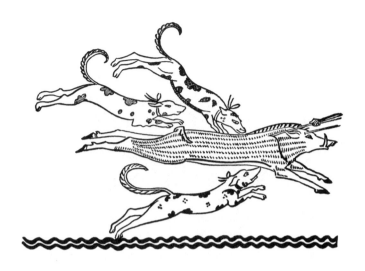

CHAPTER SIXTEEN

THE WINGS BETRAY THEIR MASTER

B y the side of a snow-water stream that gurgled its way over stones and sand from the mountaintop, three tents spread their gorgeous purple and gold, and at a respectful distance small shelters of brush and gnarled mountain timber were scattered along the hillside. Hand-woven tents, too costly even for a courtier, were a signal that royalty was present. A temporary settlement this, no fixed habitation; it was well sited in a little valley, protected against the wind, not too high for comfort and well shaded from the midday heat. On the peaks the air might be too chill for city-bred courtiers, on the plain too scorching for their delicate skins.

Beside the stream two servants washed clothes, pounding them on a flat stone, and from before the tents rose the peaceful smoke of cooking fires. Then from a distance, higher upon the mountain, came a faint sound of baying. The hunt had started, or at least the dogs were in position and had already caught trace of their quarry in the damp air of the morning.

After one isolated outburst, the baying was followed by silence, but it had sufficed to give Inas her direction. Skirting the camp and under cover of a spur of rock, she guided Ion into a little valley. Mules were better than Kadmos' speedy but clumsy-footed ponies for this sort of work, but now even Ion was a hindrance. Beyond, in the direction of the dogs, the ground was too broken to pick one's way, and the white mule would stand out against gray rocks like a white sail against the Ægean.

Inas dismounted and looked around a moment. Despite her anxiety she must find a way to plan for the animal's safety. She gave the mule a sharp slap on the flank, and twitching a reproachful ear, Ion cantered off. She would find her way to Glos' hut, or, if one of the shepherds saw her she would be picked up and taken there. They all knew her owner.

Inas turned to take her bearings. A twist in the valley hid her from the camp, but there was a chance that some followers might be out in that direction, though more probably all who were permitted would be with the hunters and the dogs. Here was grazing ground, very open, but some risk must be taken. She hurried across the wide space and was glad when she had reached the further side, scrambled through thick thorny brush, and was out upon the rocks beyond. Here sharp broken boulders appeared more difficult than they were. She balanced and leaped from rock to rock, upward and always up, hoping that she had remembered the way and that no sheer cliff would bar her progress.

The softer, older courtiers could not have come this way; they must have taken a much longer, circuitous route. Inas looked at the sun, still only two hands' breadth above the horizon. Assuming that the hunters had started at the first sign of dawn, they could still be no further than the Hill of the Three Springs.

The climb brought her out again in view of the camp. She glanced back over her left shoulder. The tents and huts were already mere specks, far below. No one could see her, or seeing, recognize her. She began to feel excitement in this rush to avert disaster. Kres's plan was obvious. What boar could find its way and of its own accord to these upland stretches? She sniffed scornfully. The plan of a goldsmith!

All country-folk knew that boars kept to low-lying marsh-lands. Had the gold worker's bitter hostility for her father, and now perhaps for her, led him to risk the king's anger by news of boar where no boar lived? If so, then the failure of the hunt might be turned to good account. Mockery was a weapon that should be particularly strong against so dignified and pompous a man as Kres.

But if, by some miracle, a boar were found—Inas swung over a hilltop, down a short valley, and began another climb—then her only hope lay in reaching the wings before Kres, by some artifice, brought them to the attention of Minos and his court.

The baying of the dogs came again, this time surprisingly close, and, as her sense of direction told her, closer still to the cave which held the glider. It was a race then? Which would reach there first? Inas—she felt her lungs laboring with the wild upward climb—or Kres?

The sheep-track by which the courtiers must have come swung across her course. Even in her haste she noticed something strange. Upturned pebbles, partly churned by feet carrying a heavy load! She wondered if Minos had so far forgotten the prowess of his ancestors that he allowed himself to be carried to the hunt, like a court beauty, in a palanquin. But further up, behind some brush, and invisible from the track, her eye caught sight of a crude framework of boughs toughly lashed together with vines. No royal palanquin, this. But a frame, constructed so that several men might share the weight of a burden too heavy for one.

Puzzled, Inas slowed in her stride, glad perhaps of the excuse to pause. She saw short lengths of rope which had been slashed through with a knife. Then sharp cuts in the springy turf and across a short patch of bare earth clear tracks of a wild boar . . . huge, bigger than she had ever seen . . . clever bait for a royal huntsman. For a gold worker Kres had so far shown much shrewdness. And by the time he wished to produce the glider from the hidden cave he would be high in royal favor.

Nothing more could be learned here. The tracks disappeared and nothing was to be gained by following them. The boar had been proved to be an actual beast . . . and what a beast! No figment of an old man's scheming brain. Proved also to Inas' satisfaction whose hand it was that had brought him here, whose command and whose gold behind the dangerous task. Now was greater need than ever for haste.

Her hand dropped to her side to make sure that her knife had not slipped from its sheath in her wild scrambles. If she could only reach the cave in time, then with a few swift strokes she could sever the lashings of the wings, bundle together the poles, fold the cloth in such a way that the reason for its presence would be unexplainable. Nothing would remain to convict Daidalos of "black magic."

To the left, just over the brow of a hill where she knew there was a thick copse of gnarled trees ringed round by close underbrush, came the sound of voices. Now she could hear the rattle of sticks on boughs as the slaves beat the thicket. Dangerous work, Inas thought, but doubtless they would be well rewarded if the hunt went according to their master's plan.

The sound of the dogs came from further to the right. There too was cover sufficient for a boar. Inas knew this well. The very next valley was the valley of the wings and this fringe of thickets encircled it. The girl halted, uncertain. To the left the beating of the thicket continued and then loud shouts and calls designed to frighten the game into the open. But to the right again sounded the bay of the dogs. With this uncertainty in the minds of the hunters, obviously the boar was still out of sight.

Should she risk discovery, show herself fully to the huntsmen, dash for the cave and destroy the wings? But in so doing, link them irrevocably with Daidalos. She hesitated a moment, deciding on the unwisdom of this. Perhaps the boar would break cover in the wrong direction and so give her better opportunity to reach the cave unseen.

As she waited a further burst of sound tore through the high air. This time not the questioning bark of dogs on the scent but the joyous, full throated peal of dogs in sight of their quarry. Three brace, four brace at least must have been slipped by their attendants. But the cheerful sound brought death to her hopes. The sound went straight down the further slope, directly toward the field where she had flown with Daidalos.

The valley of the wings, that led straight to the cave of the glider! Salute to the gold worker, for whom the gods had brought such success!

Inas swung hastily to the top of the hill. It was already deserted. The beaters had surged down after the dogs. She scrambled down the rocky slope, crossed the well-worn, well-known path she had so often taken and came out on the altar-shaped stone that overlooked the meadow and that faced the cave at the further end, in full sight of the finish of the hunt.

But she might have been Ariadne with all her maidens and still passed unnoted by the crowd below. Beneath her stretched a wide, outside ring of beaters and lesser courtiers. The center of the ring was the boar himself, a black, lunging shape before whose savage onslaught the dogs retreated, yelping, quivering, only to charge in again. The boar was at bay, growing more angry with each frustrated charge of his cruel tusks. In time he could be tired, then despatched with comparative ease, but that was not the way of the kings of Crete.

Despairing now to have the glider, for the moment Inas forgot it completely.

From the encircling ring one man stepped forward. Deukalion of the sunny smile, still with that amused expression about his curling mouth. As he moved lightly forward the ring widened, moved backward, clearly by his order. None should be near to interfere or to offer aid if the first blow of his spear should fail or the shaft shatter beneath the boar's plunging charge.

Deukalion did not hurry. Thirty paces separated him from the boar at bay. The spear was in his right hand, level with the hip. His left arm shot up in a signal, answered by a chorus of calls and clamors from the dogs' attendants. First one, then another dog was recalled from the boar, returning, well trained but reluctant, to his keeper.

Now Inas could clearly see the boar, halting, obviously puzzled by this sudden retreat of his enemies. One dog lay on the ground. The boar gave a single ripping slash to the struggling body, then turned to meet the expected attack. He stood waiting, but no dogs charged in; then he caught sight of the prince.

Inas clasped her hands so tight that the knuckles ached. This was the point toward which the entire hunt, toward which each action of man and dog had pressed; the duel between the great beast and his lone opponent.

The boar swung his head sharply to one side as if suspecting a trick. Then as Deukalion slapped his hand sharply to his thigh, the animal turned swiftly again. Would the boar charge? Inas, watching, wondered. Deukalion's was not the stiff, stocky spike designed for boar hunts, but a slender, graceful throwing spear. With this how could he possibly meet the fierce attack of a beast weighing far more than a man?

Twenty paces from the boar he waited, enough for the animal to get up full speed for his irresistible charge. Was Deukalion mad? She wanted to shout, to tell him to rush in, strike before the boar could hurl the full weight of his body in attack. So would one do with a bull.

Then the boar charged: sharp feet tearing the ground, little eyes gleaming with red anger, head lowered ready to rip and slash with furious tusks. Deukalion stood . . . stood . . . still stood. No chance to sidestep now.

At last the spear flashed forward. Deukalion leaped . . . upward, just clear of the savage, ripping tusks. The boar passed on . . . three paces, five paces. Inas could see the spear sticking between its neck and shoulders. Would he turn now on his defenseless opponent? Then of a sudden he stumbled, crashed sideways, plowed up the ground, and came to rest. Motionless. Dead!

A clamor, wild shouts rose from the courtiers. Plaudits well deserved. Deukalion raised his hand in answer and, coolly smiling as usual, walked toward the boar. All eyes were upon him for the moment, then as the shouting died and the courtiers began to turn, to drift away, suddenly the clamor began again, but on a different note.

Inas turned quickly to follow the gaze of the crowd, but knew before turning what she would see. The wings were discovered. Someone was bringing them from the cave, downhill, so it would be easy to carry that light weight. It was Kres himself, no less; Kres who had planned this perfect audience, this perfect entrance.

Then Inas noted something else and began to hope. The wind, which she had forgotten, caught under the wings, lifting them first from one side, then from the other, so that Kres staggered like a huge, drunken vulture. The feathers with which Inas had decorated the glider gave greater semblance to the absurd picture. The old man's thin legs, scraggy as those of a bird, were lifted straight off the ground as the wind caught the tight stretched cloth. Then as the glider righted and his weight hung down, his knees bent—like those of a vulture when it takes its long hop before rising.

A moan of terror rose from the watching courtiers and the dogs cowered, tails between legs. Inas almost laughed aloud. If they were frightened, what must be the feelings of Kres himself, half lifted to heaven by this strange, struggling, bird-like creature?

He was running now, not by his own volition, but as one runs whose knees give beneath him on a steep hillside. The little cliff lay just before him. Could he stop? Inas caught her breath again. No, he was over, floating in space, his legs kicking frantically, like a rabbit caught by a hawk, in terror-stricken effort to touch the ground which lay far below him.

With a bellow of fear the courtiers scattered and ran, hurtling to escape this unknown evil. Minos and the prince alone remained on the field to welcome the gold worker when he should land. But Inas did not wait; her safety also was in flight. She must not be seen, outlined here against the sky.

Bending low she scurried down the hillside and made for the thick brush which edged the meadow across which she had so lately come.

CHAPTER SEVENTEEN

ARIADNE LEAVES A MESSAGE

Her father was in danger, real danger this time. Not Minos himself could explain away the glider, could appease the fear and fury of Kres, comic as it had been.

Inas knew that the gold worker would be swift to send runners to the town to stir up further feeling against Daidalos. Men shrewd and clever and in the pay of Kres would, in the early morning, circulate through the thronged markets, the crowded squares of the city, planting a rumor here, nursing the gossip there, and, before night, even before the sun was high, Daidalos would be, in the eyes of the townsfolk, a condemned worker of dark magic, a blasphemer of the gods.

Speed was the thing. Inas wriggled skillfully through a hole in the brush, ran like a rabbit behind concealing stones that edged the open field and came to a further field. Ion was gone. Should she try to trace the little white mule? Here, in the field before her, were other mules, fresh, since they had not been ridden all night. Still, Ion was her own and would obey her. Inas stood in agonizing doubt, surveying the situation.

Picketed to pegs driven into the ground were two score of animals; black and white and cream and brown, belonging to the courtiers. There were the mule boys, down in the shelter of that big olive with its wide spreading shade. There came the sound of youthful voices, a laugh, a whistle of astonishment. Knucklebones was the attraction, and for nothing but a clap of thunder would a mule boy glance up from the absorbing game.

Inas gazed about the field. There was the great black satin-coated mule of Kres himself. Inas shook her head. That mule was as stubborn and cross-grained as his master. There was the head carpenter's small brown jenny, a sweet little beast and obedient, but hardly swift and strong enough for the task Inas had in mind. There was—she craned her neck to see better and gave a little exclamation of astonishment. Then a slow delighted smile replaced the anxiety on her face. Would she dare—would she dare!

She slithered forward like a shadow, edging her way past the hoofs of the brown jenny, past the wicked heels of the gold worker's mule, then crossed the wide, well-worn path that led to the road below. Up this path had come all the hunters, had come the palanquin of the women, had traveled Deukalion on his white stallion, Minos on the sturdy black Egyptian mare he rode on such occasions. And among these had been the light, wickerwork chariot of Kadmos' father, Meropes.

The two cream-colored ponies stood, tethered and unharnessed, in the shade of a small tree. They had been given baskets of grain and were contentedly munching, switching their full creamy tails. When Inas approached them with gentle cooing noises they looked up inquiringly, cocking nervous ears. Which should she take? The one with the black spot above his eye looked the gentler, but also, for that reason, was probably the more lazy. She'd take the pure white one with the velvet pink nose.

There was only a rope halter to guide him by, and of course no saddle. But Inas was accustomed to riding Ion without saddle or saddle cloth; surely a horse would be much the same. Gently, softly, she picked her every step lest a leaf rustle, a twig break and draw the startled attention of the boys. She need not have worried. The game was a close one and though she passed within twenty paces of the group, not a boy raised his head. The pony followed obediently in his halter. Now for the route.

If she took the main road to town she would reach Knossos long before sunset. But that way danger lay. A girl on horseback, a girl with Inas' hair, already known to half the inhabitants of the island, would be noted if not stopped before she had gone past the first sentry post on the royal road. Over the hills? That was the longer way. But time was of less consequence if she could reach the city and her own house early in the evening. Over the hills it must be.

Pulling the halter she drew the pony to a high rock and scrambled aboard. His back seemed strangely rounder than Ion's, but at least she knew he was accustomed to being ridden. Kadmos had spoken of riding him, for when Meropes had brought the horses from Egypt he had broken them to both chariot and saddle.

And then, in a moment and to her dismay, the pony seemed to go lame. Stumbling, he scrambled painfully over the rocks. He recovered his footing, but the lameness occurred again and in a different leg. She decided that the animal was not accustomed to such rough going, as were the mules, but had been driven only on the smoother highway. Probably his hoofs were very tender. That was almost the worst of the next few hours, the constant lameness and finally the extreme weariness of the little horse. He scrambled valiantly over whatever task she set him, but his whole body declared that he hated it, and what was it all about anyway?

Fortunately the path was narrow and seldom used save by the pilgrims going to offer sacrifice at the caves at Iuctus. Inas mentally checked the time of the moon. No, at this time pilgrims would be few, if any.

The pony stumbled again and she pulled her mind back with a jerk. Not until she reached the highroad, with smooth going, could she afford to remove her attention from her mount. She sighed a little. She was very weary from the excitement, from loss of sleep the night before, and from worry. Also she felt she could eat at least half a roast ox.

But try as she might she could not entirely remove her thoughts from the problem of Kres. How was she to counter the whispers of witchcraft, of black magic, which his messengers would start?

The way led steeply upward, through rocky sheep pastures where the silly black-faced rams gazed at her inquiringly, where the little frightened lambs with wagging tails scampered away. Once a shepherd called "Hae!" at her. Once a rabbit startled the pony so that she almost lost her seat. Up, up, then over the ridge of the hill. More hills ahead, but downward, scrambling and stumbling for a while. Then level ground again and the little horse broke into a trot that seemed to jolt her ribs together into a gelatin mass.

Half laughing, half sobbing, she pulled him up. "There is still no great haste," she told him and turned to reckon time by the sun. It was halfway down the sky. Another two hours and she would have coolness, and two more after that, some hope of dusk. Then along the highroad she could travel swiftly and without notice.

She tried to formulate some plan to get her idea before the people of Knossos. Obviously the best way was to spread abroad a comic tale of the gold worker's discomfiture, an amusing story of the great "kite," Daidalos' toy, which Kres, prying about Daidalos' own land, had discovered; so that Kres's messengers when they arrived with a tale of horror would be laughed out of the markets. Yes, that was the idea. And Ariadne would be the one who could help her—Ariadne, with her quick wit, her amusing tongue, and her complete command of as many traders and messengers and tale bearers as could be mustered.

By twilight they had reached the road and Inas stirred the weary pony to a shambling trot. She drew her scarf over her hair since, even in this half light, there was danger of discovery. But she passed no one on the road.

At the inn, on the outskirts of the city, Inas resolved to leave the pony that he might be returned to Meropes. Later she could explain to Kadmos. She knew there would be no trouble; the emergency had been too great. Wearily she slid from the back of the horse and straightened stiffened limbs. If she could only stop and rest here for a while, get food and drink . . . but no, there was not time. She gave a message to the puzzled innkeeper to whom she was already known, and having purchased some fruit and a handful of nuts munched them as she hurried onward through the darkened streets of Knossos.

At this hour of the night and in this sordid corner of the town there was always danger of thieves and footpads, but they would hardly suspect a hurrying girl as worthy of their attention. She scuttled through the well-known streets, dark, save for a doorway throwing a fan of light across the stones, and silent, except for occasional laughter and songs from some wine shop on the fringe of a market. She reached the wider road that led to her own house. At home she planned to stop for a time, get refreshment, and change into clean garments fit to appear before the princess. It would not be easy to enter the palace as late as this, but she would find some reason, some excuse when needed. Perhaps Teeta would have a suggestion when she understood the extreme need.

Her own house at last! At first it seemed completely dark and barred for the night. However, Inas knew a way. There was a door in the low wall to the court, but this too had been locked by the careful Teeta. Inas eyed it and sighed. Ordinarily that low wall would have been but a small obstacle. But tonight— No matter, it must be scaled.

She ran back a few paces, leaped lightly, grasped the edge and hauled herself up. Then silent as a cat she dropped to the further side. Teeta's window, opening on the yard, was still lighted. Inas stood beneath it and gave the call of the little brown owl. There was a moment's pause behind the lighted window, almost as though the Egyptian waited to verify the call, then her head appeared in the opening.

"Teeta!" called the girl. "Come down and open the door."

"I come," was the soft but immediate answer. Was there apprehension in that reply? Inas sank on the step and waited.

A moment. Another. Then a glimmer of light beneath the door, the sound of the bar slipping from its hold, and the door swung open. The little lamp in Teeta's hand threw her strong, impassive features into strange relief. Her mouth was as usual, thin and unsmiling, but her eyes were kind. She set the lamp on a table and drew the girl inside the house.

"My poor child," she said, "go straight to your bed. I will bring food."

But Inas shook her head. "Father is in great danger. I have come . . . oh, I will tell you later. Get me food now, Teeta, and while I change into other garments, fit to meet the princess, I will tell you."

"The princess?" Teeta, who had taken the lamp, set it down again. "You go to the princess tonight?"

Inas nodded wearily. "Yes, Teeta, it is of great importance. More even than I can tell you. Daidalos— But hasten, please. I must get to her soon—only Ariadne can help us now."

Teeta thought a moment. "There is a message for you. It came from the palace this morning." She slipped from the room and returned in a moment. In her hand was a sealed package, a clay tablet wrapped in vellum with a cord to bind it and on the cord the seal of Ariadne. Inas took it, wondering, slit the cord and unwrapped the tablet. It contained, on its wax surface, the fine, upright script of the princess. What could she have to say that was in such haste?

She moved closer to the lamp and read aloud: "I am going with Theseus, the Greek. The thread to the door will show him the way and I can follow to the boat below. I will take Dité with me and the gold Bull Cups. Do not grieve. I tell you first, since it is you who have helped me. In a few hours all the island will know, but you must escape the trouble this may bring upon your household. Britomartis will hear my prayers for you."

Inas dropped the tablet so that it crashed, crumbling on the stones, and covered her face with shaking hands.

"The princess! She is gone! Oh, Teeta, Teeta, what shall we do now? There is no one to help us." She buried her face on the old woman's shoulder.

It was not like Inas to break down and weep, but there had been hunger and anxiety, long hours on Ion and on the strange horse, a night without sleep and a day without food . . . and now this new unsuspected danger. It was sufficiently serious that Ariadne's support was no longer there to aid her; but in addition the princess had run away, with a Greek slave and by Inas' own suggestion and assistance.

In a few hours all would be known: Minos' favorite child and only daughter gone with a Greek, an uncouth barbarian from the north, and with them the famous Bull Cups. Any number of the palace guards might be called as witnesses that Inas had acted as go-between. And the escape through the rock doorway, a way hitherto known only to Minos, that also could be traced to Daidalos and to Inas, as would the black thread, if it were found. Inas' weary mind went round and round. All of the princess's maids had seen Ariadne give her the ball of black yarn . . . Oh, it was hopeless . . . hopeless!

Teeta unloosed the slim arms about her neck and placed the drooping girl in a chair. "Rest there," she said; and as Inas started up in alarm, "I must be off!" Teeta's firm hand pressed her back, bidding her, "Be still and wait yet a while."

Too weary to think, the girl dropped her head against the wall behind her and did as she was bidden. Just a few moments—just a few—short— She must have dozed for Teeta roused her by placing a bowl of hot milk before her.

"Here, drink of this," commanded the Egyptian. "When that is done I have ready a bath for you. Do not protest . . . I know it may waste time now, but it will save your strength and your mind for later work and planning. After that you shall eat again and we shall talk."

At first too weary to object, Inas found that her old nurse was right. Her trained body, pliant as green willow, and under no greatly prolonged strain, responded quickly to the prescribed treatment. At the end of an hour, as she sat again before warm milk, meat, fruit, and bread, she felt the glimmering of a plan for the future.

"Not long ago Minos asked my father for his own sake to leave Crete," she told the Egyptian. "Daidalos refused unless he could leave forever and under an order of exile from the king. That the king would not give but continued to urge that he . . . that we all go away for a while."

The old woman's head nodded sage understanding. On the whitewashed wall behind her a giant, shadowy head kept time to the nodding.

"Now our hand is forced. There is no other way. For a time, perhaps a year, we must remain away; till Kres is no longer in high favor, till Ariadne has returned, or till Minos' anger against us shall have had time to fade."

"There is the old brown mule in the stable," Teeta reminded her.

Inas nodded. "Father's mule is gone. Ion is with Glos. Yes, the brown mule shall take me to the cliff where I left Daidalos. Gold for the journey . . . ?"

"That is simple, I have it here." Teeta pushed forward a box she had placed on the table. "My earnings. Your father has been generous, and never since your mother's death have I needed money. Your father has given me shelter and food, and what does old age wish that gold can buy? I have here under this roof all that I need and will wait here for your return."

It was a long speech for her old nurse. Inas felt her throat close with emotion and put up a hand to hide the trembling of her mouth. In a moment she spoke again:

"I cannot thank you, Teeta, but it shall be returned. Keep the household as it is. Minos is just; perhaps his anger will not rise to

HOW MANY KNOW THAT THE PRINCESS
ARIADNE IS NO LONGER HERE?

taking our goods and property. And there is always Glos to go to. You would not come with us? No? Now for the plan."

She fumbled at her belt and took from it the leather bag containing a few small shell coins; it was not strong enough to store the gold. Spilling with the coins that rolled upon the table was a small gold ring, a little priestess, a deer with bent wavering legs, gleaming dully among the white shells.

Inas pushed it with her finger. "That, alas, is useless now— but wait, is it?" With the comfort of Teeta's listening presence she thought aloud. "How many know that the princess is no longer here? The note said, 'I tell you first.' Not yet has the court, has Minos returned from the hunt."

Without doubt no one knew as yet. The princess's ring was still a symbol of authority, must be obeyed as though she herself had given the order. Inas sprang to her feet, saw for a moment a smile of grim approval flit across the yellow features of the Egyptian.

"Teeta—" she bent to caress her— "Teeta, make ready a bundle, a few things for Father, warm clothes for me. Your food and your plan were good. I go now to act as envoy of a princess."

CHAPTER EIGHTEEN

A SHIP SAILING WEST

Perhaps it was as well for Inas that she had so little time to stop and think. Once the plan was made—and it could hardly be dignified by the name of plan, it was so problematical, so light— she must immediately carry it through. The night was passing and by morning Daidalos must be away from Crete.

"I will wait here," was Teeta's last promise. "The gods be with you." And immediately she closed the door, shutting Inas irrevocably into the darkness of the court. That also was well, for it closed hastily all delay, all roads to returning. Mufu, roused from his bed, was to come at least as far as the river with her; all the way, if she so decided it.

He walked ahead with a lantern, a small wick burning in a deep bowl swung by a chain from his hand. Inas had wrapped herself in the warmest cloak she had and carried under her arm a bundle of things for Daidalos, a coat and a few valuables together with the gold Teeta had insisted that she take.

The brown mule had been considered and rejected. Any road out of Knossos would be sure to carry now the incoming messengers of Kres, and they in turn would take report of her flight back to their master.

Mufu, unquestioning, pattered surefootedly ahead. The swing-

ing lantern made a small circle that outlined his twinkling feet
and bare brown ankles, lighted a spot of the roadway either side
of them, and was immediately swallowed by the darkness. No
voices now in any house, no lights nor sounds; but as Inas began
to descend the steep streets and felt the damp river air rise against
her face, a few lights showed along the bank of the stream. Someone called softly, a voice answered. It might be fishermen waiting
for the turn of the tide or perhaps even a ship ready to sail with
the first light of dawn.

That was what she hoped for; a ship, a big ship. Almost daily,
at this season of the year, ships sailed out of Knossos; surely one
would be sailing today. With closed eyes she made a little prayer
to Britomartis, the Sweet Maiden, then caught herself almost
asleep on her feet. Not till she reached the cliff, not till Daidalos
was away from Crete did she dare to relax into slumber.

The Kairatos was a small river broadening at high tide below
the town to make a fair harbor for shallow fishing boats and the
smaller merchant vessels. The fair, now nearly over, had attracted
many merchants to linger on past their usual sailing time; and
they had anchored for convenience close to the fairgrounds to
avoid bringing their merchandise the longer distance from the
sandy beach on the north shore.

There was a steep flight of steps cut into the rock, worn deep
by the feet of women who came laden with water, by the feet
of men loaded with bales of merchandise from the boats. Here
through the darkness Inas found her way. Mufu held the lantern
that she might see where to place her feet.

"Extinguish the light," Inas told him in a low voice. "I can
feel my way and would first see, without being seen." Already she
could tell that she would have a choice of boats; two at least, perhaps three. She felt her hand with an exploring thumb. Yes, the

ring was safely in place. Looking down toward the little bobbing lights, she wished desperately that Kadmos might be there, making ready for an early fishing trip. With Teeta she had considered sending for him, but it was too slight a chance that he might be here in Knossos or that he might fall in with her plan. She must try first this other, more desperate venture.

She reached the flat stones of the landing jetty. Three boats swung close in, one just beside the wharf, and the flickering torches, the sound of voices, the creak of shifting merchandise showed that the occupants of all were awake and probably preparing to make out with the change of tide.

The boat furthest out, Inas decided, was too small for her purpose and the people muttered together in a strange tongue. She must have native Cretans, if possible even men of Knossos, for her ring to carry full authority.

To the left a large sailing boat lay low in the water. Already its sails were being unfurled, the stone anchor at the stern was being raised. Inas hesitated, then sniffed the breeze. Here was a load of hides bound for . . . where were hides usually sent? Not far, and not to the west. Probably to the east and north. She must have a ship going west if it were to pass the cliffs for Daidalos.

The third was close in, tied to the wharf, and even as she waited a man brushed past her in the darkness and sprang aboard. He was greeted with laughter and deep voices and a torch wavered, lighting up dark bearded faces and gesturing arms. The light flared across the jetty and someone cried, "There is a woman!" And someone else laughed—"Liso has come for you, O Tachos. Best take to the river!" No doubt but these were men of Knossos. Now to determine their port.

"Hail, mariners!" she called softly. "Hail to you!"

The voices ceased, their owners listening.

"Go you to a western port, Captain?" she asked; and the answer in several tones came simultaneously, "Aye, to the west."

That was good. For a moment longer Inas paused, then whispered to the shivering Mufu, "Wait here, I will go ahead." She approached the boat. "I would speak with your captain."

There was a muttered consultation, more laughter, and the torch was again held aloft. A brawny arm was thrust across the small space between boat and wharf. "Come aboard, maiden," was the amused invitation.

Inas put her hand into the dark palm and leaped lightly. The boat was long, low against the jetty, and the water gurgled and sucked as she rocked gently, scraping against her rope fenders. A seeming tangle of ropes, oars, and bales of goods cluttered her stem; further aft a dozen men crouched or sat in the dim light. The one with the torch held it forward against Inas' face. She faced it unblinking.

Someone cried, "Why 'tis the bull-vaulting maid, she who won the fillet. Tachos, did you not win three gold coins on her brave deed in the ring?" A chorus of assents followed and Inas noted that both voices and manners contained greater respect.

"What do you wish, maiden?" The man with the torch asked kindly.

"You are the captain of this fine ship? And you sail when? With the change of the tide. Good. I wish passage, to the cliffs at the west of Knossos. There to pick up my father, Daidalos—"

"*Daidalos-s-s! Daidalos-s-s!*" The magic name slid, hissing along through the darkness. Inas continued: "See, here is the ring that gives authority to my desire." She held her hand out into the full flaring light of the torch.

He who called himself captain bent forward in the torchlight and several other dark, tangled heads peered closer. "The princess's signet!" That whisper also was passed along the length of the ship. The captain, troubled, hesitated a moment. "We go within the hour, with the first streak of light."

Inas nodded, "I know, that is good." Should she, she wondered, send Mufu back? She decided suddenly that it would be wiser as well as more comfortable to take him with her. "I have a servant here," she added.

"We have little room for passengers, and no comforts," he warned her.

"No matter. Still I wish it."

The captain shrugged, "It is the command." He seemed indifferent. "But who will pay?"

Not wise, perhaps, to let these men know that she carried money . . . "My father is wealthy—"

A murmur of agreement came from the men. Yes, that was well known. The captain made a gesture toward the dark bow of the boat. "Tell your servant, then, to come aboard. You will find a rough blanket there. One of our men is delayed and we must sail without him."

In a moment Mufu, shivering, half with cold and half with fear, had tucked Inas into her cloak and the unfolded blanket. The captain picked his way forward to tell them that the tide had already turned, that soon, in a few moments, they would be away. There were shouts and orders, the rattle of the sail as it was slowly raised to place. For a little time Inas struggled desperately against sleep, then murmured to Mufu, "Waken me when the sun is just above the horizon," and she sank down, down, into delicious darkness.

It was seemingly only a moment later when she was aware of a peculiar scratching sound below her ear. She brushed it away with a drowsy hand. Oh, how she wanted to remain asleep! The scratching came again . . . and again. At last she dragged open one eye, expecting darkness as before but the light was that of full mid-morning. Immediately remembrance flooded back to her. She sat up, flinging off her coat. Mufu had wakened her by scratching on the boards beside her ear.

Both sails were set and they must have been out of the harbor for some time. Squinting through the sunlight toward the mainland at her left Inas tried to recognize some of her surroundings and for a moment her heart seemed to stand still at the thought they might already have passed the cliffs. Then not far ahead she saw the caves, and struggling free of her wrappings she gave them and her bundle to the boy. She picked her way aft, past the chattering sailors who rested on their shipped oars. Now that the wind was fair they had no need to labor.

Inas found the captain—dark, wiry, with matted hair, half Phenician, by his hooked nose and full lips—at his place in the stern, and said, with outward firmness, "There are the cliffs where we shall find Daidalos. Soon you must lower sail."

No time must be lost. She knew that even now the gold worker's strange tale of the wings would be buzzing through the markets and squares of Knossos, that even at this moment Minos must have heard of Theseus' escape from the Labyrinth, of Ariadne's flight.

The captain shook his head. "The winds are favorable for a swift passage, the rocks and currents are bad at this spot. We cannot put in here."

With apparent absent-mindedness, Inas caressed the ring on her finger. "Minos will be angry—" she began slowly. Two or three of the sailors had turned to listen to the talk. Now there was a faint murmur of assent at her words. Minos indeed would be angry if this symbol of his power failed to exact obedience.

And their own families and their property were in the city of Knossos, under his rule.

"If you do not stop here as you promised, then I shall dive and swim ashore," threatened Inas desperately.

"And then Minos will be without his favorite bull-vaulter." One of the sailors, indicating the waves sweeping high on the rocks to the south, had become an unexpected ally.

"No boat could put in here," objected the captain. But Inas persisted: "There is a small beach, just around that next point. It is only stones and pebbles and it is sheltered from the waves. I can land there, make my way up the path to the cliff, bring Daidalos back with me. I shall be gone but a few moments."

The captain hesitated, slanted long black eyes toward the ring that gleamed on Inas' finger, then shrugged. "If this beach is as you say—" he began, then turned to give an order for lowering the sails. There must, however, be no delay, he told her, else he would make off without either Inas or her father. With knees shaking with relief, the girl made her way back toward Mufu. In any case she must go ashore here.

But once around the bend of the cove, in full sight of the narrow beach, a surprise awaited them—Daidalos himself standing on the shore, the wreck of a glider, mere broken sticks and tattered, water-soaked canvas in his hands. His clothes were drenched and as the boat drew nearer Inas could see a jagged cut running from thigh to ankle.

He glanced up as the boat swung round the bend, and Inas called, waving wildly. "Father!" she shouted above the crash of the waves. "Daidalos!"

"We can go no closer," reported the captain.

"No matter. I can swim from here and Daidalos will return with me. He also was a bull-vaulter," Inas reminded them. She poised for a moment on the gunwale, then went overboard in a clean dive. The water was cold and she came up gasping, but with a clearer head than she had had for the past day. In a moment she had pattered up the short beach.

"Father, you must come quickly. There is no time to explain." She put a hand on his arm. "We must flee, there is real danger this time; no mere affair of poisoned honey. So much has happened, I cannot explain here."

He let fall the wreckage of the glider and glanced down at his blood-stained leg. "You ask me to flee and I can, at the moment, scarcely walk a step." Inas saw that the leg was badly bruised. Possibly he had fallen against the rocks just above.

"No, not that way—" she looked at the cliffs just above them— "but by the ship. Mufu is with us. I have money, clothing, and the captain says we are stocked with sufficient food. All has been thought of, even Teeta. But Ariadne has gone, escaped with her Greek, Theseus, through the secret door in the Labyrinth. Yes—" at Daidalos' exclamation—"we—I shall be blamed for it. I put a thread there, as clue to the doorway, since Ariadne asked me to. I had thought that only Theseus would use it, and without doubt he is too stupid to think of removing it afterward. You must come with me, truly."

Daidalos' face had sobered, was suddenly almost old. "Yes, my child, I will come." Without further discussion he limped into the water. His lips were tight as the salt stung the wound on his leg, but he swam steadily, strongly toward the boat which the sailors, with their long oars held in position.

Shortly they were aboard again and the sails, like wings unfolding, rattled into place overhead. Forward, Mufu had shifted bales and spread out coats to make a corner of privacy and seclusion. Inas bandaged the wound on her father's leg, using strips from her tunic, the edge torn from her cloak. The salt water had cleansed the cut.

"And where are we bound for now?" he asked at last.

Lying back against the dipping bow, Inas shook her head wearily. "Now it is in your hands. So much has happened. There was a boar hunt . . . at the valley of the wings . . . and Kres discovered the glider," she told him briefly. "Minos was there also, and Deukalion. All things have been against us lately."

"It is not important," he soothed her. "I think you have been wise and strong. Sleep now, for you need it. I will tell the captain to land us at Zafare, at the western end of the island. There we can hide for a time, a few days or a few months, and return when Minos and the people again have need of me."

Inas rolled her cloak into a pillow. For a while the sails would serve as a pleasant shade, and indeed she was very weary; then glancing backward toward the cliffs, she uttered a little cry.

Heads bobbing, figures moving, even along the lower cliff below the caves. Already Kres's messengers had had their effect. What would have happened if Daidalos had remained, even a little longer, there on the beach? She shivered at the thought.

"I think, daughter," remarked Daidalos, his eyes following the diminishing figures, "that my danger was even greater than yours. Now sleep. We are safe here."

CHAPTER NINETEEN

THE LAND OF THE SICELI

Inas surveyed the long gray shore half hidden by the early morning fog, the long gray breakers on the sloping, rocky beach. Impossible that here, at last, was where they were to land! Days and nights, more days and nights than she had cared to count, had slid behind them since Crete had disappeared, blotted out by slanting lines of rain. They had huddled together; Daidalos with characteristic stoicism, Mufu unwhimpering but with bluing lips and chattering teeth, Inas with growing indifference and boredom in the scant space allotted them in the bow of the ship. A wretched voyage, she decided, and wondered no longer that Kadmos was always so glad to return to Crete. But perhaps all voyages were not like this one.

There had been delays and adverse winds. Twice on the trip, as they had stopped for cargoes at other ports, Daidalos might have gone ashore, chosen that place to be his future home. But since the gods had willed that wind and storm should not allow them to land on the western end of Crete, as he had hoped, he seemed to have made other plans. Was this perhaps what he had hoped for?

What was this place? Inas wondered and glanced aft, toward the captain. He stood astride a rowing seat, ordering the lowering of the sail, the manning of the oars.

Daidalos, wakening, raised himself on one arm. Here at least something good had come from the voyage, for with the rest and forced idleness his leg was well healed, though still stiff and lame from lack of exercise. In answer to his inquiry one of the sailors answered:

"This will be Sicelia, the land of the Siceli, and the city hidden now behind the fog is Kamikos, ruled over by Kokalos. You will find Cretans here, and the land once paid tribute to Minos."

Inas had heard of the Siceli and their great land, far greater in size than Crete. Oh, it would be good to walk once more on firm ground, to run and dance, to eat something besides salt meat and dry bread, to drink water without a flavor of goatskin, to bathe once more . . . she was almost sure she would be happy here.

With a hae! . . . hae! . . . hae! the sailors lifted high their long oars, hung for an instant over the gray swell, then plunged forward to land far up in shallow water. Instantly every man was overboard, struggling knee-deep against the swirling undertow, shoulder to the ship's bright painted sides. Up . . . up, muscles straining, every face twisted with the terrific exertion. And at last the ship lay far enough out of the water so that the next backward sucking wave would not sweep her out to sea again. She must be unloaded before she could be completely beached.

Inas scrambled to her feet and went over the side, Mufu close at her heels. Daidalos followed more slowly, his leg still feeble from long inactivity. He stumbled on the rock-strewn sand and Inas gave him a strong young shoulder.

"Oh, I feel as though I could run and shout. Land . . . land again!" she cried thankfully.

Daidalos nodded in understanding. "Soon I shall send a message to the king; I think he will welcome us here. What is this, fresh water?"

For the sailors, once ashore, had started digging in the sand, small cuplike holes a few paces back from the mark left by the last high tide. Left alone for a short space, the cup filled slowly with water. Inas bent to taste it, fresh as any mountain spring. How strange to find fresh water here, so close to the sea!

Small fires of seaweed and driftwood were lighted, an early fisherman came with fresh fish to sell and this first meal of the morning was spiced with cheerful hunger. By the time the bones were picked an audience had gathered: ragged urchins from the town to the north, a few women who had come to fetch water from the small wells along the shore, some fishermen and early traders, all jabbering in a polyglot speech, part Cretan, part something else unknown to Inas. These people lacked the fine-toned slenderness of true Cretans; their bodies were heavy, clumsy, large boned, their waists lacking the slimness required of the true inhabitant of Knossos.

Daidalos called for the captain of the boat and sent him, somewhat unwilling, with a message to the king. When that had been despatched he ordered Inas to wash as best she could, to arrange her tangled hair and put her salt-stained clothes in the best order possible. "For soon we shall meet with Kokalos."

Wondering, Inas went to do as she was told, but Daidalos' prediction was a true one. Blue sky had scarcely broken through the early fog, the beach was only beginning to warm with sunlight, when a small guard of soldiers, very gay in bright uniforms and glittering bronze helmets, arrived under the command of the captain of the palace guards. They brought a message of welcome to the famous Cretan, the greatest engineer and magician of his age, and came to escort him to an instant audience with the king.

Inas saw that the sailors were whispering together, knew that they were again impressed by this man they had brought to Ko-kalos, who was about to be honored by a great king, and she stepped proudly beside him up the pathway to the city gates. But she wished that she might have been dressed more fittingly, in, perhaps, her geranium gown with its high collar, its embroidered jacket and full skirts. This sea-stained cloak and worn tunic were no garb to wear before a king, especially if that king had daughters.

Inas had never seen a fortified town before and the grim walls encircling the city seemed terribly prison-like as she heard the gate shut behind her. The town, like Knossos, overlooked the sea, but there the resemblance ended. The streets were dark and dirty, the houses low, leaning shoulder to shoulder as they did in the older Knossos; but here were no sparkling fountains, no wide open squares, no gay bright colored frescoes of flying-fishes and dancing girls. The palace itself was cold and gray and more prison-like even than the city. She tried to be grateful that they were at last on land, free of the pitiless rain and scorching sun of the past weeks, tried to be glad that her father would here receive the reception he deserved, but she shivered when she looked about her.

So, while the Great Green Turtle that nibbles the moon ate slowly through the shining disk, and during the subsequent period of darkness—while another was being made anew for him, only to grow larger and larger—and in the early days of his attack on the new disk, Inas lived in the walled city above the sea. She was free to come and go as she chose, to explore along the windy, bleak rocks that edged the shore, to wander through the markets and streets of the town, to talk to shepherds and fishermen. Only Daidalos was held a prisoner, though not unwillingly.

That he was held at all and in any such manner, Inas discovered only by accident and after they had been some time in Kamikos. One evening they were walking along the high rocks that led down to the boats, and there happened that day to have come a boat from Mycenæ, a port north of Crete which paid tribute to Minos. Inas had recognized the smaller blue octopus, as compared to the large black one of the Minoan Fleet, and cried gladly, "Oh, Father, here will be word from Crete, people who speak our own tongue!" For to Inas the accent of the palace was uncouth, outlandish, and harsh to the ear.

Daidalos smiled. "Run, if you wish, and talk to the men from the ship. I—I—" he glanced behind him along the rocks. Inas followed his eyes and for the first time noted three tall Siceli, garbed in leather jackets and armed with spears, who appeared to loiter behind them.

"What are they doing, those men?" she asked; and then at her father's expression, "You don't mean—!"

"The King of Kamikos puts a high value on his new engineer. But do not concern yourself," he remarked dryly. "I have no wish to escape."

To Inas that seemed the worst part of it. Bad enough that her father should be guarded like . . . like a priceless slave, but horrible that he should not wish to escape.

The king had given him every possible convenience for his work: a high stone chamber with a forge and a boy to work it, whatever instruments he wished, raw materials, and had even listened with extreme interest to Daidalos' tale of his attempts to fly. The engineer had been promised aid and space for further experiments, as well as protection from any superstitious fears these might arouse among the natives of the town. Inas realized that her father was not an old man, that his life, vigorous and full of promise, still lay before him, and here at last was a king who knew the value of his, Daidalos', great genius. She could hardly blame her father for being content here even in a kind of exalted slavery.

But for herself it was different. The king had three daughters, Elymis, Hykkas, and Chalca, all older than Inas and all, so far, unwed. That seemed not strange to the Cretan girl. They were to her unattractive women, heavily built with thick ankles and wrists, with minds as heavy and sluggish as their untrained bodies; they seemed content to sit all day gossiping over the loom or telling pointless tales while they twirled their spindle whorls.

For a while Inas had been treated as an honored guest. Then as she and Daidalos became more accustomed to the ways of the palace, they were accepted as almost a permanent part of the king's own household. This was seemingly a great honor, but Inas had preferred it when she was left more to herself. Now she was given tasks to do and had discovered that her hours along the shore, spearing fish or paddling, lonely but quite contented, in the blue water of a little quiet inlet, were sadly curtailed.

"Today," she told her father one evening in his workshop, "I disgraced the fair island of Crete and all its women!"

Daidalos was working on a tiny clay model of the city of Kamikos; every street, every open square, every block of houses in its exact place as though seen from overhead by a giant bird. With this, he told Inas, he hoped to show the king where lay its weakness in fortification, in the grouping of the markets, in the primitive drainage. Now he modeled a tiny bridge in clay and set it across a miniature mimic stream.

"How, disgraced?" he asked.

Inas laughed shortly and settled herself on a table, her back against the wall. "Elymis has three times set up the loom for me and started me on the weaving. Twice I have made such a fish-net tangle of the threads that she told me good material was thrown to waste. Today—" Inas yawned lustily as though the very thought of it added to her boredom, "today, she started me again and spent a weary morning in showing me how to throw the shuttle, how to pound down the woof that it may lie firm and even. Oh, Father, why am I so clumsy with these womanly things? Is it because I'd far rather always wear a leather jacket than weave fine material all day in a dim room?"

"And then what happened?" asked Daidalos quietly and rolled clay between his palms to make a thin long cord which he sliced into tiny bricks.

"They talk and talk, the princesses and their maids. Gossip of this and that, long-winded tales of how this queen looked when laid in state on her death bed, and of how the women wailed along the wall when that king died; just such stuff as Ariadne's maidens told, save that the names are different . . . and oh, their voices! They make merry over mine; saying my accent must be affected and not my own." She minced her words as the Princess Chalca might have said them. "They ask me many questions of Minos and Ariadne but only that they may jeer and mock and say, 'Why, how strange! It is not thus we behave in Kamikos!'

"And at the end—" she laughed again but there were tears behind the laughter—"I drew my knife. No woman in this city wears a knife, it is deemed unwomanly. They were frightened, but I only slashed the warp of the loom, then turned six cartwheels from the chamber! *Aiee . . .*" She put her hands over her face and the bitter tears of homesickness trickled out between her fingers.

Daidalos dropped his work and came across to put his hands over hers, to draw her head down on his shoulder until her sobs had ceased. "My child, my child! I have been selfish. But truly, all this will soon be in the past. Minos will not leave us here for long, and you shall have your wish to return to Crete. Have patience just a little longer."

And indeed it was not much longer. One afternoon Inas escaped from her distaff and loom, and with Mufu at her heels, ran out to roam along the rocks beyond the town. There, above the small quiet bay where she went to swim, was a high point which overlooked the harbor and the sea beyond. Below her, in the bay, rocked a little boat. Inas spied it with delight. It was a roughly built fishing boat but still a boat. Would it be too big for Mufu and herself to handle alone? Might she borrow it for an hour's sail—the sea was very smooth today—and be back without discovery?

She clambered down the rocks, shed the heavy full-skirted Siceli costume which she now wore and poised for a dive into the sea.

"Wait here for me, Mufu," she directed. "I will bring the boat back," and Mufu, grinning from the high rock above, sat down to wait.

The sea was warm today, but Inas did not linger. She swam with long strong strokes to the little boat, hauled herself aboard and could have wept for homesickness as she did it. Almost the last time, the last two times she had stepped thus aboard a sailing boat, Kadmos had been there to reach a welcoming hand.

The craft was strong and seaworthy, equipped with a small sail, and Inas found, stored away in a small place forward, two skins of fresh water, fishing lines, and a cache of hard-baked bread. This very day, someone had provisioned the boat for a fishing trip. The craft would hold five, possibly six men. Inas looked about for the oars but found none and wondered if she could manage the clumsy sail alone.

"Mufu!" she called and stood up again. The boy got to his feet and cast a casual glance over his shoulder, then stood as though he had sent down roots.

"Mufu!" Inas called sharply again. Then, "What is it? What do you see?"

Mufu, with pointing finger and eyes big with astonishment, was gabbling some unintelligible nonsense about something he saw on the rocks beyond or perhaps on the water beyond the rocks.

Inas shouted again, but found she could get no sense from him; so, puzzled and exasperated, decided to go and see for herself. She dived once more, came up beside the rock and climbed into the sunlight above, then followed Mufu's enraptured gaze.

Not far at sea, just beyond the line of breaking whitecaps, showed another line of white; sails that caught the sun in tiny, snowy, glistening patches. In advance of the line one boat alone arrogantly rode the long rollers; and even as Inas watched, the men leaped overside into shallow water, began to draw her up to the beach. Her prow glittered with gold and across her gleaming sail sprawled the black octopus, symbol of Minos himself.

Inas felt her throat swell with emotion. Minos, the king of Crete, had come for Daidalos. Oh glorious, glorious! All would be well now, all would be as it was before and they could go home! She must race, race back to meet the ships. Friends would be there, and there would be the sound of her own tongue spoken as she herself spoke it. Inas scrambled into her discarded garments, gave at least three contradictory orders to the bewildered Mufu, and with damp hair streaming in the breeze raced to the palace.

The way seemed intolerably long. Once she was delayed maddeningly, by a band of sheep across the road, once by a half-dozen laden, stubborn donkeys which blocked the narrow path along the rocks. Not until she reached the palace, tore up the steps, shoved through the great bronze-sheeted doors did another thought occur to her. Minos might not have come in friendship.

She stood still then, listening. From the broad way that led to the main entrance came the skirl of bagpipes and roll of drums. Minos' own guard. Kokalos even now must be receiving him. Up a well-known back stairway, down a corridor, past her father's workshop—Inas paused again. If one of the princesses should meet her! Inas made a wry face, adjusted the cloak about her shoulders, patted her drying disheveled hair into some order.

Then ahead of her, standing alone in the late afternoon light that streamed through a deep window, she saw a familiar dark head, a beloved figure, and raced to throw herself into its arms.

Kadmos!

CHAPTER TWENTY

THE WOODEN WALLS OF CRETE

"Kadmos! My almost-brother!" How big he looked, how strong and brown, and oh, how beautifully *Cretan*! Also he seemed as glad to be here with her as she to have him.

When the exclamations were over, when each had expressed surprise and delight at seeing the other, she slipped her hand into his arm. "Come! Come with me and tell me news of Crete! Has Ariadne returned? And have you seen Teeta? And—"

But Daidalos, coming quietly behind them, stopped them with a harsh command. "This is no time," he said, "for gossip." Inas, who had never before heard her father speak so sternly, felt again that shiver of apprehension she had known when she entered the palace and glanced at him questioningly.

"Follow me," commanded Daidalos, "to my workshop here."

And as the boy protested that he was in Minos' train, had been posted here and must not leave, Daidalos stressed his order. "You must indeed. It is of great importance." He led the way to his own apartment, looking back each moment, anxiously as though afraid Kadmos might vanish even while he turned his head away. Once inside his door he closed it, shot the bar, demanding, "Now tell me quickly. Why is Minos here?"

Kadmos' face was worried. "I do not know, sir. But the king was very angry. Huge rewards were offered for your person and for Inas here. Then at last word came back that you had fled to Kokalos and that you were even now making new wonders for the king of the Siceli." He described how and in what haste the Fleet had been made ready and sailed. "Minos means to have you back, but whether as friend or foe I cannot tell."

Daidalos shook his head sadly. "It is no use. You must go, both of you. Alone I cannot save the Cretan Fleet, and Minos—" he shivered slightly and his face was pale. "Inas," he turned to the girl, "you have been free to wander about the town and the harbor. Do you know a way out of the city, could you find a road by which to escape, a boat to take you?"

"But, sir," Kadmos broke in eagerly, "if you wish Inas to return with me, and do not wish to go yourself, might not she return on my ship? I am a captain now, of Minos' Fleet." Pride rang in his voice and Inas too was proud of the honor. But what did her father mean? Not go with her?

"I can never leave here. Nor can— But no matter. Take the girl and go quickly. If all is well, then you can return. I give her into your care. Here she is not happy. Take her back to Crete, make her your wife; Meropes and I had always planned it so but not in this manner. But I chatter like an old woman. Go now, and hasten."

Inas flung her arms around Daidalos' neck and would have lingered in farewell but her father put her off. "No time to stay, I tell you," and with many orders as to a heavy cloak, food, and Mufu, Daidalos bundled them from the room. Wondering, they obeyed him, though reluctantly.

As they hurried down the deserted halls even Inas, torn between a dozen concerns, felt the tenseness in the great stone palace. All was quiet. No sentry guarded the way she had come in, but as they circled to avoid the silent crowd that waited at the outer gate she noticed a line of Cretan soldiers, the half-dozen who had come in attendance on Minos.

"Minos must be already with King Kokalos," Inas panted as they raced along the rocks below.

"Kokalos sent words of welcome," Kadmos spoke in snatches, "offering Minos all hospitality and refreshment after his long voyage." No true Cretan would resist such an offer of comfort and ease, but Inas remembered the three princesses, with their dark, implacable faces. And Kokalos had no love for the king of the great Cretan empire.

They came out at last on the little promontory from which Mufu had first glimpsed the Fleet, and Inas stopped there to look back. The beach where the Fleet had drawn up was hidden by the rocks, but below her Mufu, confused by her conflicting orders, had waited and watched the boat.

"Fresh water," she told Kadmos. "Yes, and food. It is as though the gods had planned it," and they picked their way down, in the fast dimming light. Mufu was the one who discovered the oars cached in a crevice in the rocks. That indeed was a find.

Hardly knowing what to think, Inas took her place in the stern. There was no breeze here. Besides, it would be wiser to row for a time; a sail showed so far in this slanting sunset light. She wondered whose boat this was and if the owner's loss would be great, and wished she had thought to put a gold piece where the fisherman might find it. But Daidalos, once the word had reached him, would compensate for that. The sun dropped behind the hill and they drew slowly out to sea.

"Here we can drift for a time and then if all goes well, put in and join the Fleet," Kadmos suggested. But Inas shook her head.

"I feel that something is wrong," she said unhappily. "I know not what to do." Then she asked, with a lighter note, "And Ariadne, is she returned to Crete?"

Kadmos laughed shortly. "The princess? No, nor ever will. Word has come that she is wedded to the Greek. Folk say he is chief of a small band of half-savage herdsmen near a place called Sparta, or mayhap Athens."

Inas wondered if Ariadne could be happy there. How strange it was that she should be here, and Ariadne so far away. She turned the little ring on her finger and fell thoughtful and silent. All the gladness seemed to have melted from this meeting with Kadmos.

"What is that strange sound?" The boy's voice broke through her thoughts and she listened while they waited, leaning on the oars. The sea, like a sheet of gray metal, reflected luridly the last bar of sunset light behind the town, and where the Fleet waited a fire flared suddenly, and across the water came a low rumble like many voices shouting together.

But Inas, listening, heard another sound farther off, higher, as from the palace walls. Eerie, sad, and at the same time triumphant, like some strange night-bird, it sounded; and for a moment the growing flares along the beach and the sound of shouting died beneath that high, strange call.

Women, wailing from the walls! Where had Inas heard that spoken of? They had said—"when a great king dies"—but who would die, there?

"*Minos!*" she cried suddenly. "Minos is *dead!*"

Kadmos turned a face pale in the dimness, to gaze at her. "And they are firing the boats along the shore! I must go, I must go!" He bent frenziedly to the oars, but Inas cried, "Stop, you cannot go!"

"I, too, am a soldier; I cannot see my men slaughtered like sheep, without a leader."

"Daidalos must have known of this. Minos was doomed from the moment he set foot within those dreadful walls. It is because of this that Daidalos sent me with you. Oh . . . don't you see . . ."

The light flared redder, higher. Shouts, hoarse yells, the clash of bronze on bronze came out across the blood red water. Kadmos again rested on his oars, his face troubled, unhappy.

Inas said nothing, but waited, her eyes on Kadmos' face. Again he struggled with the oars, but the tide was running out and he made little headway against it. Smoke from the resin-calked ships rose heavily upward, obscuring the last of the sunset light, and the smell of the resinous pitch came floating on the breeze. The faint wind that had carried them so quickly from the shore was now against them. The sea, once red in the sunset, had turned brown in the smoke-filtered light, then darker without even a silvery ripple, so that they scarcely noted the moving blob upon the water till it was close to the boat. It was when the dark patch changed its direction, started perhaps to swim away again, that Inas cried out:

"See, Kadmos, something there upon the water."

"'Tis a man," Kadmos decided after a moment, "a man, swimming from the fight." He raised his voice in a hail.

The object paused and seemed to sink slightly on the gray water. Inas added her voice to the call and the head turned and came slowly toward them. As the face appeared close to the boat's side they could see the man was too spent to speak. Kadmos shipped his oars and while Inas balanced the boat, Mufu and Kadmos dragged the swimmer aboard.

For a moment he lay gasping in the bottom of the boat, then raising his head, "By your speech, true Cretans," he cried. "Praise be to Rhea!" He struggled to raise himself higher on one arm and through the darkness scanned his rescuers for confirmation. "All, all is ended," he said at last. "Minos is dead, the Fleet is burned. All are dead save I, who am wounded and likely to die, and you whom I see before me, if indeed you are true Cretans?" His voice rose a little with renewed anxiety. Inas reassured him and he turned his gaze to examine the small vessel. "A boat of Siceli," he said at last, "such as would go on no long voyages."

Kadmos broke in: "All cannot be lost, all dead. Such fighting would last till midnight—later. Hark!" Still the subdued murmur which they knew now must be the shout and roar of battle reached them over the still harbor. Flames were shooting higher, but still the tide carried them further from the shore.

"'Minos is dead,' so said the king of this city, bidding us of the Fleet to go in peace. But when we would not, behold our ships flamed behind us. Carry me but to Crete, and all that I have shall be yours." The soldier gasped and sank backward against Inas' knees.

"Carry a coward to Crete and leave brave men fighting, dying, behind you?" Kadmos' tone carried with it all the scorn he must have felt for his own plight, and his hands on the oars quickened their struggle against the seaward tide.

Inas saw his expression, guessed his emotion. "A fool would

indeed join in the fight and die, a wise man do his duty and carry news with all haste to Crete." But Inas too looked longingly back at the battle. "Now that the Fleet is gone, the wooden walls of Crete no longer stand. Before our enemies have word of our help-lessness and prepare their attack, word must be borne to Deuka-lion, and the defenses put in order. Perhaps it is this that Daidalos foresaw when he bade us flee."

Kadmos, who had waited for the end of her speech, nodded reluctant, grim assent. Slowly, with a backward look toward the flames that died along the beach, he laid by his oars, freed the sail of its encumbrances, grasped a rope. Seeing his gesture, Inas signed to Mufu to add his weight. Slowly and with creakings the sail rose to the masthead. The boat rounded, pointed again toward the east and the gathering darkness.

Inas drew closer to Kadmos. "A long voyage, Captain, with only a girl, a wounded man, and a slave for crew."

CHAPTER TWENTY-ONE

THE DIVINER'S PREDICTION

Not willingly, after it had ended, did they speak of that voyage. Despite their utmost economy, water gave out soon after the food. Once they caught water in a cloak, from a sudden shower. Three times driven by hard necessity, they put in at the nearest land to take on water and purchase supplies; twice, as strangers, barely escaped with their lives. At last they reached the cove beneath the cliff where Inas had once descended like a great bird on Kadmos and his *Sea Raven*.

Here should be rest and sanctuary. For days they had talked of this homecoming. Floating on dark seas, they had looked forward to warm firelight, bright lamplight. Sipping stale, flat water with a strong flavor of goatskin, they had thought of great drafts of clear cold spring water. And munching the last bits of moldy bread, all that remained of what had been purchased at the one place they were allowed to land, they had dreamed of great oxen, roasted whole over an outdoor fire, of delicious mutton, dripping delectable juices into the hot embers, of cakes and tarts and of fish baked in the glowing coals, not eaten raw from the sea. All, all was to be as it had been in the past, in the days before the bull-vaulting, in the days before Inas had seemed to tempt the gods to try the temper of her courage.

Leaving Mufu to guard the boat, Kadmos and Inas, with the wounded man between them, struggled up the narrow goat path which seemed so much steeper than it had been in the old days; up, up till they reached, in the last light of evening, the meadow below the cave. Here the soldier could walk unaided, and here Inas clutched fearfully at Kadmos' arm.

"Behold, a light! A light in the cave!" Who could know of this hidden place?

Kadmos placed a firm hand across her lips, signing for silence, signed too that she should wait while he went on ahead. A brief moment and he returned, Glos appearing behind him in the lighted doorway.

"It is only Glos, the shepherd, but I bring bad news. The country house of Daidalos was burned by the people after the boar hunt. For this reason Glos withdrew here, with his sheep and such things as he could rescue from the flames."

To Inas this additional misfortune seemed of complete unimportance. She made a gesture of weariness. "No matter, here is food and water and a place to rest. Come with me." She led the two men toward the cave. "Glos shall descend with food and drink for Mufu in the boat."

For a little while they rested there. The cave was deliciously warm and bright with firelight, and even the smell of the sheep, crowded into the place that Glos had fenced off for them, was a pleasant, homely smell. Then Kadmos, somewhat refreshed by the mere change from the crowded, rocking boat, borrowed a cloak from Glos and insisted that he must press on to the town. His was a trust, to take news to Deukalion of his royal father's death.

"And you too must go." Inas turned to the shepherd. Now that her father was no longer in Crete, all Daidalos' slaves and lands belonged by right to her, and hers was the responsibility. "I must have word of Teeta and of the men and maids under her care."

Grumbling, as was his habit, but not entirely unwilling, Glos departed with Kadmos and the wounded soldier. The latter had insisted that he make his way as far as a settlement close by, that there he had friends with whom he could stay. Inas let him go without protest. She could understand that any of the four might be glad to see no more of the others for a time.

For her the night passed in troubled sleep. She would lie before the fire, half drowsing, to feel the boat still rocking, rocking, then start fully awake, aware of the stillness about her, the small scrape of hoof on stone, the breathing of the sheep, the crackle of the fire, glad to know that the other had been just a dream. Toward daylight, however, having slept so badly, she decided to see if all was well with the little craft. She crept out, to find the sky a sheet of rosy sunrise, the air fresh, the sea calm, and walked across the grassy meadow to the edge of the cliff.

Below her, Mufu, with such coverings as Glos had taken him and the warm food, had made himself comfortable. Curled in the boat he slept soundly. How peaceful was all this, and how good to be on one's own land again! Soon everything would be almost as it was before. Except for Daidalos . . . and Meropes? For the first time Inas remembered Kadmos' father. Had he too perished when the Fleet was burned at Kamikos? Kadmos had said nothing, but surely the commander of the Fleet would have been there.

The sunrise had lost its bloom for her and she returned to the cave. The sheep must remain folded till Glos should return, which would be shortly. Kadmos would probably remain all day in the town, arrive with news that night. Inas did not dare to appear in Knossos till she had some word of the feeling there. Indirectly even the death of Minos might be laid to her.

She found food in the cave, and with the morning meal over, looked for something else to occupy her mind and hands. Mufu, once more examined, still slept in exhaustion. Back in the cave again, she looked about and found a pair of gliders, the second pair that Glos had brought from the valley of the wings. They had been partly rebuilt by Daidalos, on some new plan. A few more strappings of heavy cord and one linen wing put into place, made them again ready for use. Inas finished the task and took them out to the edge of the cliff, overlooking the little boat and Mufu. She tested the wind which, after sunrise, had begun to blow strongly from the northeast. If no one came, if no one was in sight, she would try the wings again, once more descend on the waves below. That at least would serve to pass the time.

Then she heard voices approaching along the upper cliff and placed the gliders behind a scrubby bush. Was this Glos coming back? And who was with him? Teeta, surprisingly enough, and Kadmos, whom she had not expected until evening.

"Teeta! Dear Teeta!" Inas ran to welcome the old Egyptian and found both Teeta and Glos strangely laden with bundles and parcels.

"Ion, with a further load, is back at a shepherd's hut," Teeta told her. "No more shall I return to Knossos."

That was news indeed but more was to follow. Once word of the disaster at Kamikos had reached the town, spreading like a dry-season fire among brush, Kadmos had become almost a fugitive. "Renegade Kadmos! How happens it that he alone, of all our brave sons, has escaped? How happens it that he has returned?" So ran the word from lip to lip.

Deukalion, who had heard the whole story and who was overwhelmed with grief, had immediately exonerated him, had even sent a messenger with such word among the people. But as usual the tale had already grown and spread out of all semblance to the truth of the happening. Kadmos was even branded as a spy who had betrayed the Cretan Fleet to the king of the Siceli. Bitterly disillusioned, he had barely escaped without a public stoning, and meeting with Teeta and Glos upon the road had joined them to return to the cave.

Teeta sniffed at the breakfast Inas had prepared, but sat down to eat with the others. Once that was disposed of, Inas thought it wise to call for suggestions and plans.

"I cannot return to Knossos," she told them, "and it is evident that Kadmos also is much out of favor. You, Teeta, declare that you are finished with the town forever, and Glos here—" She glanced questioningly at the old shepherd, who as usual was scowlingly silent.

"There is still the boat," Inas continued, "and though I am sick to death of ships and seas, still it seems safer than the city. Teeta, Mufu, Glos, Kadmos, and myself." She checked them on her fingers. Yes, it would be possible to get them all aboard, and there were places far nearer than Kamikos where they could take refuge. She wondered if Glos would insist that his herd of sheep be not left behind.

Teeta rose briskly. "Is there fresh water aboard this craft of yours? Food for the voyage? No. Then let the men make her ready for the trip." She hustled them from the cave. There was a good spring nearby. With the help of Mufu, two or three trips down the goat path should make the craft ready again.

"But truly, Teeta," Inas told the Egyptian, once they were alone in the cave, "I know not where to turn, where we shall go. There are many dependencies of Crete where we might be welcome, until news reached them of our fortunes here. Then—"

It was then that Teeta came forward with her bit of counsel. "Go join the princess Ariadne," she suggested. "While you were gone a tablet came, brought secretly by a traveling merchant who had stopped at Sparta. The princess sent greetings to you and told you of her happiness with Theseus."

Inas, who was putting coarse flour into a water-tight skin she had found in the cave, paused in surprise. "This tablet, where is it, then?"

"Such was the message upon it," was Teeta's firm reply.

"But Teeta—" Inas stopped, helplessly. Who had read the message?

"I read it," Teeta answered the unspoken question. All these years the Egyptian had been quite able to read and write. Inas thought she would never fully understand this strange old woman.

The men, returning for another load to stock the boat, had further disturbing news. A fleet of unknown ships, too far yet for the symbols on their sails to be read, had been spied off the coast to the west.

"The lion is dead, already the vultures gather to the feast," Kadmos said grimly. "Had Minos consented to fortify more than the north gate of the city—" and he shouldered another sack of food for the boat.

When he returned again it was with word that the ships were

fast approaching. "And time must not be wasted." He took command. "Teeta here, and Glos, must go down to the boat. Mufu is ready and will hold it in close to the shore. As soon as the ships, whatever they are, have rounded the cliff that hides us from the town, we can get away. A small fishing boat will never be noted."

Inas nodded. Yes, that seemed a good plan, but Glos for the first time broke his morning's silence. He did not intend to leave Crete. Unexpectedly Teeta joined forces with him. She too was content to stay here.

"Kadmos' duty lies with his promised bride," she said. "But we two are too old for change. No matter who comes to rule over us, we common folk live much the same. It is the mighty ones such as Daidalos and Minos that fall. For us there are always the hills and the sheep, and the gods are always there."

Glos gave her an approving glance and grunted words that may have meant she was welcome to what he had to share. Through all her trouble, Inas was glad of this. Surely it was the wisest way.

"Nothing more remains to be done." Kadmos considered the two. "Perhaps you will be safer here, happier, than in a strange new land. Bide here, then, if you will. Come, Inas." He had indeed taken command.

Inas made her farewells. It was hard to leave the old ones, yet impossible to believe that she would not, soon, see them again. Glos' harsh voice became inarticulate. Teeta alone remained unmoved. "Go, and the gods go with you."

Still gazing behind her, Inas rounded the entrance to the cave, then turned to see Kadmos, with an anxious frown on his face, searching the rim of the cliff top above them.

"There, and there again." He pointed with one hand, drew the girl down behind the cover of a rock. "Those are not sheep but people. Listen!"

The cliff edge cut off individual sounds but clear on the breeze came the ominous buzz of human voices, angry voices. A mob; the horrible inhuman menace she had heard once before, when the hue and cry had pursued them through the fair. Inas knew it again now, knew once more the desperate fear of a hunted animal.

Now those figures had found the path down the cliff, were beginning to descend, more pouring down behind them. Red points of light flashed from polished bronze spear-heads, from high-held swords, and Inas felt a fresh surge of fear. Whom else could this human pack be hunting but herself, daughter of Daidalos, whom they had come to fear and hate, and Kadmos, who had brought a proud people word of its defeat?

Now one of the pursuers was pointing. Yes, there could be no doubt. She seized Kadmos' hand. "Come, let us run!"

"Where?" Almost angrily he shook her off. "On the cliff path to the boat we shall be picked off like flies upon a wall."

They stood up now, in full view of the pursuers. With a desperate scheme seething in her mind, Inas started to run toward the cliff edge above the water. Behind her Kadmos hailed the oncoming mob. No greeting was returned, only the clamor grew louder. Threats, wild yells of approaching triumph, came to her as she ran.

As a man, Kadmos would wish to stay and fight. Only by running could she make him run also, to be with her and protect her at the end. But agonizingly she listened for his footsteps. Would they never follow?

The shouts were nearer still when his footfalls pounded behind her, drew level. "Run, Inas!" he counseled. "I will guard the cliff edge while you descend. Not for nothing have I fought with the Fleet in many lands. These city folk—"

"There is a better way," she panted. Using her utmost speed she drew ahead of him, came first to the glider. What fortune had made her assemble it? The wind buffeted her face as she stepped in the open space between the wings. No chance to slide her arms through the loops; her weight must be forward of them to leave room for Kadmos. Her outstretched fingers grasped the ribs of the wings, raised the glider from the ground, though it tore and twisted in her grasp. Then Kadmos steadied it.

"Make haste," she panted. "Do as I do."

Quickly he inserted his body into the same open space, his chest tight against her back, his arms spread out like hers over the wings.

"Now, together, the few steps to the edge. Run!" Clumsily they stumbled forward, so clumsily that the tail of the glider barely cleared the cliff's edge. And they were in space.

There had been no time to make delicate adjustment of balance, either that balance was right, or—The nose dived steeply. Inas threw back her legs, her body. Kadmos with swift understanding followed suit. Now they were on even keel, seeming for a moment to float motionless, but dropping lower, riding out from the cliff.

Their pursuers had reached the cliff edge; the two were even able to hear wild shouts of rage. Doubtless some were scrambling down the long cliff path, though Inas had no chance to turn her head and see.

"By Britomartis, this is adventure! Never have I felt such fear." Kadmos' tones were thrilled, however, not afraid. Inas tilted her feet a little forward now. The boat, with Mufu, showed clearly on the sunlit water just beneath them. As well not to overreach it since, with Kadmos as passenger, it might be impossible to turn and spiral back.

"When we strike water, see that you do not become entangled," Inas counseled, and an instant later the sea seemed to swoop up to meet them. Feet first, they struck, and landed on their faces.

Inas felt Kadmos' chin or nose hit the back of her head. As the wings struck water she released her grasp, sank beneath to swim up clear of the wreckage. Kadmos' head appeared beside hers. The boat was not twenty strokes away, rocking at her anchor, and Mufu, crouching in the bottom, gazed with enormous frightened eyes over the gunwale.

"Mufu!" shouted Kadmos. "Mufu! Haul up the anchor," and emphasized his order by a ferocious wave of a wet arm out of the water. Mufu scrambled to obey, and by the time Kadmos had hauled himself aboard and reached once more an arm as aid to Inas, the little craft had started to drift slowly out to sea.

Together they raced to raise the sail. Mufu, moving quickly for once, began to pole with the long oar. Perhaps his movements were hastened by a spent spear which clattered harmlessly but none the less threateningly against the side of the boat.

A moment more and they were out of range of any spear, no matter how strongly thrown, and Inas drew a deep breath of relief. It was just as they rounded the cove for the last time that her gaze turned back, half longingly, toward Knossos.

A dense cloud of smoke lit by lurid darting flames hung like a curtain over that once fair city. Moment by moment the cloud grew denser and a distant roar, thousands of voices intermingling dreadfully, came softly over the still water. Already a few boats, too small to have been caught within the net of the raiders, were putting out to sea.

Inas turned her face away. There was nothing more that

she could do. She could only hope that somehow Crete might emerge, victorious, as always.

Mufu curled himself in the bottom of the boat to sleep again. The sun was warm; they had fresh water, food; Kadmos was with her. Where they were going she did not know, could not guess, but suddenly she remembered a vision, told by a diviner long ago in the palace of a happy princess.

"I see you and a youth in a small boat on a sunny sea. You land in Greece—and a princess rises to meet you there."

She uttered a little prayer to Britomartis that the diviner might have told truly.

AFTERWORD

No one to this day knows who were the mysterious raiders that, in the absence of the Fleet, burned Knossos and the other great towns of Crete. It came with terrible suddenness, that raid. Three thousand five hundred years later archæologists, digging on the site of the ancient city, came upon jars of oil in the palace hall where some slave had been filling smaller vessels from a large one, came upon a gold worker's bench, with tools that had been dropped in flight, and a carpenter's tools hidden hastily in a cranny in the wall. But they found no clue as to who the raiders might have been.

For many centuries Minos and Knossos were lost to history. Homer makes some reference to Minos, but the civilization Homer portrays is of a different people: the clothes are different; the weapons are strange; food, manners, and customs are all of a different type; and iron is beginning to become known, whereas the ancient Cretans had only bronze.

Most of our knowledge of ancient Crete we owe to one man, Sir Arthur Evans, who has written a three volume book on the palace of Minos and who has superintended a large proportion of the excavations at Knossos. In 1900 he became part owner of the site of the ancient city, and since then other companies of archæologists, American, British, French, and Greek, have excavated and tabulated other sites on the little island. Just two years ago a learned man in Oxford attempted to prove that the language of Minos and of Daidalos was the background of the Basque tongue, and that the Basques, who live today in a small corner of France and Spain, are the modern descendants of those ancient people.

There are several other fascinating books about the people of Knossos. *Minoans, Phillistans and Greeks*, by A. R. Burn, is among the best, and *The Ægean Civilization*, by Gustave Glotz. Then H. R. Hall has written two, *The Oldest Civilization of Greece*, and *Ægean Archæology*. The Encyclopædia Britannica has excellent material on this subject; look especially under "Crete" and "Minos." And there is a beautiful room full of reproductions of the frescoes, of the jewelry and the sacred Bull Cups, in the Metropolitan Museum in New York. There are pictures of the Vaphio cups in many books and reproductions of them in the Museum. These were discovered years ago at Vaphio, which is near Sparta, so they are named after the place in which they were found; yet there is no doubt that they were among the finest works of Knossos goldsmiths.

Knossos was never rebuilt in its former glory. The empire died with the burning of the city, and though a few inhabitants crept back to camp listlessly in the ruins of the town, most of the inhabitants seem to have fled north to the Minoan settlements along the coast. There for a time Cretan art and gold work lingered, but weakened, without vitality.

No one yet knows the language of ancient Knossos, but through the Greeks we have inherited a few words, undoubtedly with the Cretan characteristics: "Labyrinth, narcissus (narkissos), Cynthia, Hyacinth, abyss." These few faint whispers, some broken bits of lovely pottery, a few restored frescoes, and a small heap of gold work—such are all that remain of one of the greatest empires the world has ever known.

LIST OF DECORATIONS

The decorations are redrawn from murals and decorations of Knossos and other Minoan cities.

Chapter Seven. Griffin: from the restoration of the throne-room

Chapter Eight. Head of a prince: from a palace fresco

Chapter Nine. Bull-vaulting: from a palace fresco. (The men were conventionally represented with very dark skins, the women with pure white.)

Chapter Ten. Minoan lady: from a fresco at Thebes
Bull caught by vaulter while drinking at a trough: from a seal

Chapter Eleven. Bull's head, in silver with gold-plated horns, and the sacred double ax: from excavations in Crete

Chapter Twelve. Double ax pattern: from a Minoan jar

Chapter Thirteen. Boy with rhyton, a vessel for ceremonial oil: from a palace fresco

Chapter Fourteen. "The Captain of the Blacks": from a palace fresco. In the wall painting this man leads a group of soldiers.

Chapter Fifteen. Man with horse and dog: from a palace fresco

Chapter Sixteen. Boar chase: from a fresco

Chapter Seventeen. The seal ring of "Ariadne": adapted from a ring in the author's possession

Chapter Eighteen. Cretan ships: adaptation from a Cretan pattern

Chapter Nineteen. Flying-fishes: mural from the palace at Knossos

Chapter Twenty. Young prince and soldier: from a cup found at Hagia Triada, another populous city of ancient Crete, also recently excavated

Chapter Twenty-One. Libations by priestesses and a priest at the altar of the sacred double ax: from a decorated sarcophagus

AN APPRECIATION

BETSY BIRD

She dives deep into the sea to collect sponges and braves shark-infested waters to meet a friend's boat. With a breathtaking combination of skill and accuracy she backflips over bulls, toys with the notion of killing a shark by hand, and hops into home-made hang-gliders when the need arises. Living as she does in Crete during the Minoan period (around thirty-five hundred years ago) you might think of her as a kind of acrobatic Cretan superheroine. When push comes to shove, Katniss Everdeen has nothing on Inas, daughter of Daidalos.

Never mind that her book was first published more than eighty years ago.

I spent the better part of my early days as a young children's librarian working my way through the established canon of American children's literature, supplementing award winners with popular contemporary titles, classics, and anything else that caught my fancy. While shelving materials in the college where I took my library school classes, I stumbled upon an old but fairly pristine edition of a book called *The Winged Girl of Knossos*. Something about the title and the fact that it was a reinterpretation of the Icarus/Daedalus myth appealed to me. I checked it out, took it home, and started reading.

The first words state, clear as crystal:

BEFORE THE STORY BEGINS

Long, long before blind Homer sang his songs of ancient Troy, long even before Troy itself rose from the ashes of her past and fair Helen smiled from the towers of Ilium, Minos reigned in Crete.

The author, Erick Berry, adopts the voice of the storyteller, conjuring the history of a lost civilization. She toys with the reader, suggesting that perhaps Crete of long ago was, in fact, the lost island of Atlantis. More questions than answers spring up, as Berry enthralls with her telling. Yet, beneath it all, she takes care to draw our attention to the kernel of truth that can enable even the wildest of storytelling. The book says, "[B]eneath the stony soil of Crete, palaces vaster than those of Troy, ruins greater than those of ancient Athens, and remains of a people that was old in culture when the fair-haired Achæans, clad in skins, tended their flocks on bleak hillsides, and crouched over their half-raw meat in primitive huts of mud-plastered logs." So too, deep beneath the myths and legends we associate with the Greeks, the truth about the real Minoans of long ago is a treasure itself.

As I dove deep into Berry's tale I was struck, like many readers who have stumbled upon this book in the decades since its publication, by how modern the voice and the writing felt. Anyone who has slogged through old Newbery Award– and Medal– winners can attest to the fact that there is often a stilted quality to even the finest book. We somehow expect our older children's literature to be stodgy and overbearing, riddled with didacticism and outdated mores. Not so, *Winged Girl*. This is not to say the book doesn't contain outdated and sometimes offensive racial stereotypes. It does, though happily they are few and far between. Overall, however, with its remarkable heroine and thrilling plot, the book feels as if it could have been written pretty recently. So why is it largely forgotten today?

For years this Newbery Award–winner has remained out-of-print. As a result we know fairly little about it. We know that "Erick Berry" was a pen name for author Allena Champlin Best, who lived from 1892 to 1974. Born in New Bedford, Massachusetts, to a reference librarian and his wife, she would go on to write and/or illustrate around one hundred books for children. Of these books, the one best remembered is *The Winged Girl of Knossos*. Today, Best's papers are housed in the magnificent de Grummond Children's Literature Collection at the University of Southern Mississippi. There you will find her correspondence, scrapbooks, and material on twenty-six of her titles but, unfortunately, not much about her best-remembered book.

Sometimes information about an author comes from an unexpected source. In 2008, the respected author and children's book blogger Peter Sieruta discovered some interesting background information on *Winged Girl*. As he wrote on his site, *Collecting Children's Books*:

> I also had a letter written by Erick Berry, which I stumbled across in a bookstore some years ago. Addressed to a book reviewer who'd written a favorable critique of Berry's *Juma of the Hills*, the letter includes a plug for a couple of Herbert Best books (in private life, Erick Berry was Mrs. Herbert Best . . . though she neglects to mention that fact in her letter). The note also reveals that Harcourt had turned down her latest manuscript. Since the book Berry published after *Juma* was *Winged Girl of Knossos*,

and it marked her move from Harcourt to Appleton-Century, I can only assume that *Winged Girl* was the manuscript that Harcourt rejected.

Yet, even the highest honor for a work of children's fiction—the Newbery Medal—can't guarantee lasting fame for an author or her book.

When it was written, *Winged Girl* was part of a movement to portray girls as more than mere pretty faces. Inas was to presage an entire line of independent heroines in Newbery Award books. Before her 1934 win, the heroines of the 1930s Newberys included the ultimate passive protagonist, the doll Hitty from Rachel Field's *Hitty, Her First Hundred Years*, followed by the male heroes and boy adventurers of *The Cat Who Went to Heaven* by Elizabeth Coatsworth (1931), *Waterless Mountain* by Laura Adam Armer (1932), and *Young Fu of the Upper Yangtze* by Elizabeth Lewis.

Then came 1933 and with it an impressive nine Newbery Honors, including *Winged Girl*. Berry's classic was bested in the end by *Invincible Louisa: The Story of the Author of Little Women* by Cornelia Meigs, another tale of a strong, independent female. One need only look at the books that won Newbery Awards in the years to come to see that Berry and Meigs paved the way for a whole new breed of heroines. *Caddie Woodlawn* by Carol Ryrie Brink (1936), *Roller Skates* by Ruth Sawyer (1937), and *Thimble Summer* by Elizabeth Enright (1939) portray girls as capable of conducting independent midnight rides, solo roller skating missions, and cartwheels whenever the fancy strikes. They wear overalls and reject the cultural norms of their time, celebrating a kind of freedom many women could only experience in childhood, before society pulled them into the fold.

Reading a short description of the book, a person could be forgiven for thinking Inas but a pale imitation of Icarus. Instead, she is a brilliant, gender-swapped reimagining. If Inas were to fly too close to the sun it would be because she wanted to experience the fall firsthand. Look, for example, at the moment we first meet her. With a trident under her arm, her toes gripping a stone sinker that will plunge her into the depths, she gives the signal, and when that stone goes down the book makes it very clear that Inas keeps her eyes open all the while. She always keeps her eyes wide open. And Inas doesn't engage in this dangerous activity for profit but entirely for sport. Hers is a life of calculated risks. Calculated, I say, because she loves risk and is willing to do anything for her family and friends. And if it happens she must do something death-defying in the process? All the better. Ultimately she is the one who saves the day. Though she is accompanied at the story's end by a man sworn to protect her, she not only figures out how to use his bull-headedness to her advantage, but she also devises the plan that saves the two of them from certain death at the hands of a mob.

Erick Berry did not intend to write a character who could inspire generations of women. Berry makes it clear from the start that her purpose is to inspire readers to wonder about the island of Crete—its glory, its destruction, and its legacy. That part of the book may speak to some young readers today as well. After all, this re-publication could not be better timed. Who could have predicted that a generation of American schoolchildren would come to learn about the Greeks, their myths and their legends, thanks in large part to Rick Riordan's Percy Jackson series? Or that comic book artists like George O'Connor would tell the story of Daedalus, Theseus, and the Minotaur through the art of the graphic novel? Many child and teen readers today are well

versed in their classical myths, so it seems all the more appropri-
ate that they see how much original storytelling can be gleaned
from something that is both so ancient and yet still so relatable.

For too long this book has been overlooked. It brings me
great joy to see it back in print. Hopefully whole new generations of readers—girls and boys—will come to love and appreciate
Inas and her many fine adventures in a time and place from long
ago. I could not wish them a better companion or a more worthy
inspiration.

Hae, Britomartis!

ABOUT THE AUTHOR

Erick Berry was born Allena Champlin in New Bedford, Massachusetts in 1892. She spent her childhood in Albany, New York where she attended Albany Academy for Girls. Her father was the reference librarian in the State Library of Albany and gave Berry her first interest in books. Her first art training was at the Eric Pape School in Boston. This school was run along the revolutionary lines of the Paris studios, and Berry was so influenced by Eric Pape that she later acquired the name of Erick when she attended the Pennsylvania Academy of Fine Arts. When she married Carroll Berry, the artist, in 1916 her pseudonym became complete.

Berry completed school and tried her hand at various undertakings, including miniatures, murals, syndicated newspaper advertisements, designing of toys, Christmas cards, and department store fashions. Eventually she traveled to Paris where she studied art and later made her way down the west coast of Africa. In Nigeria she met and married her second husband, Herbert Best, who was a British government officer. Her first two books, *Black Folk Tales: Retold from the Haussa of Northern Nigeria, West Africa* (1928) and *Girls in Africa* (1928), resulted from her African adventures and enabled her to become a member of the Women Geographers. Berry and her husband began their collaboration as author-artist, with Berry illustrating all of Herbert Best's children's books and most of her own.

Berry wrote and/or illustrated close to one hundred books for children. She wrote and illustrated *Winged Girl of Knossos* (1933) for which she received a Newbery Honor award in 1934. She also illustrated two titles, *Apprentice of Florence* (1933) and *Garram the Hunter, a Boy of the Hill Tribes* (1930), which were Newbery Honor winners in 1934 and 1931 respectively. Berry and her husband lived for a time in the English Devonshire country, on a farm in the heart of the Adirondack Mountains, in Jamaica, the British West Indies, and sometimes spent winters on the eastern shore of Oahu. In later years they made their home in Sharon, Connecticut until Berry's death in 1974 and Herbert Best's death in 1980.

—From the Erick Berry Papers, de Grummond Children's Literature Collection, McCain Library & Archives, The University of Southern Mississippi